Shadowed Heart

Shadowed Heart

LAURA FLORAND

Chapter 1

H appiness, Luc thought as he stroked his wife's bare shoulder, was not like chocolate. It didn't melt if you held it too long in your hands.

He lowered his head to her nape, a profound ease spreading through his muscles as he breathed in her scent—coconut and tiare from the monoï oil she still used, to carry the scent of the tropics with her everywhere.

Happiness was not like spun sugar. His fingers spread her golden hair over the pillow, a net of tangled silk. It didn't shatter if your fingers held it a fraction too tightly. It let you play with it forever and never grew too brittle for touch.

The light from the bathroom cast his shadow over Summer's gold.

He lowered that shadow, spreading it all over her to capture her gold for his as he braced his arm. He loved this moment—when his body skimmed hers in so many places, just barely held separate from hers, so many tiny contacts vibrating through him, waking greedy hungers for more.

Because happiness wasn't like anything he worked with at all. It wouldn't get marred if he gripped it too hard sometimes and held it to him too tightly.

His happiness, in fact, would probably like it. His lips curved at the thought of how much, as he brought his lips to brush just lightly over the corner of her sleep-parted ones, hunger growing. Because it turned out his happiness did have one thing in common with his work— he could eat it all up and still make more of it tonight.

Summer's eyes blinked open, and she rolled the rest of the way over onto her back, her lips forming a sleepy invitation for another kiss. In the growing light of dawn, he could almost make out the blue of her eyes.

The growing light of dawn?

His head lifted. 6:00 AM glowed by the bedside in green digits. Oh, shit, he was already late. He had to catch his damn fruit supplier and personally strangle him.

He pressed a firm kiss on Summer's lips and leapt from the bed, running a hand over himself to straighten his clothes as he headed for the door. That was what he got for letting himself get distracted when he stopped to kiss his wife good-bye.

Thank God happiness was different from anything else he had ever known or worked with in his life.

Thank God that sometimes, if he needed to, he could even save it for later. He paused at the door to look back at his wife. "I love you. I'm sorry, it's just—" He gestured to himself, to the door. To the insane demands of this new restaurant that he was trying to get off the ground, so that they could make their new home here in Provence, this happy, sun-filled country that he had never known.

"I know." Still sleepy, she made a little reassuring gesture with her hand, as if she was petting his worries away, and shook her head, smiling at him. "I'll come in after I get a shower."

He hesitated. "You don't have to. I can handle it by myself." *I can handle anything. By myself.* That was always the best way to handle things. "I don't *need* you." God, that was such a stupid lie. Why did he keep trying to tell it? Sometimes, when he tried to do accounts himself instead of relying on her, it felt like the damn spreadsheet program was going to leap out of the screen with monster teeth and eat him alive.

Something flickered in her expression, but then it was gone. And she shook her head again, with another smile. "I like to help, Luc."

Was he a strong enough man for her, if he needed her help? But he found himself smiling at her, despite the pressure of that growing light and all its demands on him. "I love you," he said again.

Those had to be the sweetest damn words in the world. Except for possibly—

"I love you, too, Luc."

Yeah. Those ones. Those were the absolute sweetest.

So he had to keep deserving them. He blew her a kiss and hurried out the door.

As a child, he'd once had a cardboard box in which he kept all his happiness—a toy found abandoned in the Métro, a bracelet a little girl gave him in a park. A box marked all over with scary monster faces to keep away anyone who would want to steal its contents.

He couldn't keep Summer in a box. He'd like to, but then she wouldn't be happy herself. So he took deep breaths as he walked away from her, toward his restaurant. He insisted on believing in them with each and every breath.

Because it was counterintuitive. It didn't correspond with anything else he had ever learned in his life. But thank God it was true that sometimes his happiness would keep.

***

Summer lay back again in the bed, lingering in the slide of Egyptian cotton sheets, gazing out the huge window onto the Mediterranean far below. It was a long way from a shack on a remote South Pacific island to a luxury home on the Côte d'Azur—a long way *back*, as if her pampered and lovelorn childhood kept reaching hands out of her past to try to grab her and drag her down again—but she had Luc this time. And she had the strength in herself that she had built in those four years on the island, four years when she had escaped from her heiress lifestyle to become someone of value, someone who mattered.

So even though it was lonely, and even though she had yet to find a single friend and had to pretend the restaurant staff were her friends, their life here was not going to be anything like her childhood at all.

And she had an appointment. She rested her hand on her belly.

Best not to get Luc's hopes up until she knew for sure, because it would turn him into a basket case. He would get so excited in that intense, incredulous way he reacted to happiness, and so crushed—in that contained, back-behind-shields way he reacted to disappointment—if those hopes were dashed.

She'd wait until she knew for sure, until Luc wasn't caught up in the restaurant and had a chance to focus. Because after all, if it was what she thought it was, the news would keep.

Maybe.

She caressed her belly curiously, hopefully, even warily.

She was trying to be strong, and she was trying not to whine and wish for her island friends, but if she was right about what the doctor was going to say, she wasn't entirely sure she could handle this news all by herself.

Chapter 2

It was midnight before Luc stepped out of the kitchens into that still unfamiliar and lovely Provençal alley behind the restaurant, flexing his shoulders, rolling his head, his eyes closing just a moment as he took a deep breath of cool night air and jasmine and clean stone, trying to ease the stress out. God, what a night. He missed his team in Paris so damn bad.

Patrick, *merde*. What he wouldn't give to have his old *second* Patrick down here, all laughing pseudo-surfer attitude and intense skill, helping him get this restaurant running right. Instead of helping with the transition to a new chef at the Leucé sixty hours a week and buried in his math and physics summer courses another twenty, trying to build up the foundation to start an engineering degree.

Engineering. Luc had tried and tried to wrap his mind around that as a career for Patrick, but he couldn't even entirely imagine what an engineer would *do*. From everything he'd read, it sounded like what he and Patrick already did, only with a lot more boring materials.

And with permanence. There was that.

So he'd lost Patrick—to one of his own interns, a black-haired woman named Sarah—and to another dream. One that had permanence.

And now he had everything on his shoulders, every single aspect of making sure this *worked*, that one of the wealthiest and most beautiful heiresses on the planet hadn't married a failure. That the sweetest, shyest pseudo-socialite hadn't bravely left her island and come into his harsh world for nothing.

He couldn't be nothing again. For her sake, he couldn't be nothing.

He was used to refusing to be nothing for his *own* sake, and to have it instead be for her, to have had his whole world shifted so that he was no longer his own center but she was, left him radically off-balance. But he was doing his best.

And his best was the best in the world, damn it. It was.

But right now...the compressor in the walk-in had failed, putting thousands of dollars of food stuff at immediate risk, not to mention that it would have shut them down for days if the supplies got ruined and couldn't be replaced. So he'd spent an hour frantically calling around in a strange region—the Parisian snob chef whom no one local quite wanted to help—trying to find someone who could fix it at that hour of the night. His chef de cuisine, Nico, from the area, had stepped in and made a few calls and someone had shown up a half hour later, which would have been fine, except that normally the executive head chef *was* a chef de cuisine, not a pastry chef, and Luc had to establish his authority and power absolutely for the staff to accept the reversal of the roles. He couldn't be the person who failed to solve a problem that his chef de cuisine could solve with a couple of calls.

Then his night dishwasher and his night porter were acting as if they were about to knife each other, and he had no idea why. That was the kind of personal dispute that Patrick had always solved. His new sous-chef, Antoine, just didn't seem to have the knack yet.

Summer, actually, had an odd knack for it. But since most of his staff was in love with her and would do anything to make her smile at them, it was a knack that made him want to strangle every one of them. And Summer had taken the afternoon off and hadn't come back in for the dinner service. He'd missed her. This great hole opened in his life when she wasn't there, and he had to remind himself that he was a sane adult man and not that obsessive, clinging brat that kept clamoring back from his childhood.

6

Not everyone wanted to spend every waking moment in a restaurant. It was fine.

He had to do payroll tomorrow morning, unless he let Summer do it for him, but he couldn't inflict that on his own wife. Payroll, God. All the bits and pieces of working hours, who had covered for whom, who had worked a double shift, who was flat-out lying about the hours he claimed. At the Hôtel de Leucé, sure he had to keep things in order in his part of the kitchen, but the hotel had had *accountants*. Good ones, too. In the end, he could shove it over to them.

Here, like everything else, it was all on him. The math of it was already giving him a migraine, and he'd downed eight aspirin already tonight.

Fuck.

"Let me," a warm, husky voice said, and his eyes flew open.

"Summer." He tried to relax all the tension out of his shoulders as he turned toward her. She couldn't see this. How hard this was. How intensely he fought to succeed.

Perfection costs me nothing. Of course not. It's just the way I am.

Which, if it were true, would make me almost worth you. That fragile, generous, wanting heart of yours that you let me hold.

He smiled at her, happiness seeping through all those tense muscles and unwinding them in an involuntary way far more powerful than all his efforts to force the relaxation.

"Here." Summer reached her hands up to grip his shoulders, digging her fingers in, and he gazed down at that beautiful face that was all his. Delicate but strong cheekbones, sunlight hair, blue eyes, fingers trying so hard to be strong enough to really ease his muscles.

Because she was so much smaller than he was, she couldn't really dig into his muscles properly from her position, but...the effort accomplished quite a lot. Her fingers finally shifted from the attempts at massage to stroke gently up and down the nape of his neck. Pleasure ran through him, this shivering deep sensation of slightly too cold water after a much too hot day. He would ease into it in a second. His body would accept it, be delighted with it, just as soon as it had a chance to adjust to the fact that it was actually his.

"I'll give you a better massage when you get home and can stretch out," Summer said. A tiny flicker in her eyes, the most fleeting look. "Do you think you'll get home soon?"

A knot of tension came back, even under her hands. "I'm trying," he said. "I'm sorry."

He knew it was one of the things she had most feared from him, that he would pour himself into his work just as her self-made billionaire father had and forget to leave her any worth or room in his life at all. He'd promised not to be like her father.

"It's okay, Luc." She stroked his cheeks. "I know. I know getting it off the ground is hard."

She always said that. She always seemed okay.

Okay being the one to make all the efforts for them to see each other. Okay coming into the restaurant to fold napkins and set tables and act as hostess when their new staff once again failed to show up. Okay stopping by the restaurant late at night like this just to talk to him a minute and rub his shoulders. Okay being the person who poured out all her support with a smile and never, ever asked for a single thing back.

But Summer was so good at faking things to try to please. Had any other man ever thought she was okay with him right up until he was staring at that golden hair as she walked away?

"I love you so much," he murmured, closing her back against the stone wall of the old building, mostly just to cage her. *Mine, mine, all mine.*

His hand fisted around the jasmine climbing up the wall. The building had been used in the eighteenth and nineteenth centuries to process the flowers harvested in the region, and in some spots inside it, away from the kitchens, he could swear he still caught hints of rose and lavender when he rested his head close to a wall. But here, in the Provençal night, he could only smell stone and jasmine and her monoï-based shampoo. It was like smelling the essence of starlight.

"I'll finish up as soon as I can," he told her, bending down to kiss her.

But she brought her hands to his shoulders and pushed him back, and because he was stupid, he had to work not to tense at even that tiniest rejection. "I have some news." Her eyes, big in the dim light, made her look almost scared to tell him. "I was trying to wait until you got home, but I just couldn't wait anymore."

Something she was excited about, then. The school had finally said she could volunteer? He caught one of her hands on his shoulders and squeezed it while he bit the words back just in case that *wasn't* her news. She never talked about how hard she had worked to try to get any school around here to let her teach or even volunteer, and how many people had turned her down as if she herself, minus money, was worthless. Probably she didn't want to make him feel bad for dragging her here.

For dragging her away from that island, where she was so happy and confident and valued, to his world, where people treated her like some very expensive shit. She'd known what it would be like, and she'd still made that choice. For him.

"Yes?" he nudged when she didn't speak. Squeezing her hand again, he rubbed one thumb down over her knuckles.

Her eyes got so huge he could drown in them. She took a deep breath and then let the words out fast, on a gasp: "I'm pregnant."

Chapter 3

The world stopped.

Right there. Frozen with one of his hands in jasmine, with his forearm pressed against stone, with his wife in the cage of his body, with her hand trapped by his against his shoulder.

His world froze so still that all he could do was stare at the image of himself in the pupils of her eyes, black hair against black, lit only by the light from the kitchens, so that he seemed shadowed by some darker self. The great glass shadow of a self he had to look away from in the mirror, or in any great dark window shutting out the night.

Hell. He was supposed to be looking into her eyes to see *her*, not concentrating on himself.

"You're—what?" Breath forced its way between the two words, awkward and choppy. His hand crushed the jasmine.

She took a gasping breath and smiled the biggest smile in the world. But blue, night-darkened eyes clung to his as if every single thing depended on him.

So he had to get this right.

"You're *pregnant*?" His gaze ran down her body to her belly, but it looked just exactly the same. Slim. Impossible to fit a baby in there. "Really?"

She beamed and nodded, but her eyes still clung to his. Still waiting for him to do the right thing.

"My God." Something was happening to his hearing. The world seemed to be pressing up close to his ears and receding in this strange pulsing confusion. This great golden swelling of joy and this dense, gray contraction of fear, over and over. "Really?"

He wanted to kneel down and stare at her belly. But he was suddenly afraid to touch it.

"It's due in February," she said. Their baby would be born only thirteen months after they first met.

"Wow," he whispered. He'd wanted her to get pregnant so bad. *Four black-haired kids, playing with us in lavender fields. We're going to be so happy. Trust me. Trust me with you.*

Trust us.

Trust me not to let this happiness shatter or melt.

Let me have it all.

"That's wonderful." He couldn't get his ears to stop ringing, and the echo of his voice sounded tinny and strange. From the kitchen, pots clanged loudly as the *plongeurs* attacked the last great batch of the evening's dishes.

"I know!" she exclaimed. But over her smile of happiness, she looked nervous. Her eyes were still clinging to his, as if he could produce miracles.

Well, he *could* produce miracles. But not this kind of miracle. Not without her. He looked back at her belly wonderingly. One of his cells was in there, creating something so incredible with hers?

"Oh, wow," he said again softly.

Oh, good God, they were going to have a baby.

A father. He was going to be a *father?*

Oh, hell, what did he know about *that?*

"Wow, Summer." He took her hips, carefully, squeezing them. It was the closest his courage could get to her actual belly. That belly where two tiny cells had joined together and made him a father.

"Isn't it?" Her fingers kneaded into his shoulders as her eyes searched his face.

Pregnant.

In a hammock in the South Pacific, he'd first created this tropical lagoon of a dream for them: four black-haired children, eternal bliss, them wandering hand in hand. Under southern stars, cradled in a hammock swinging by an aqua sea, they'd drawn gorgeous visions of happily ever after.

It felt as if that tropical lagoon had just risen up in one great tsunami wave and knocked him flat.

"That's wonderful," he said. Had he just said that?

Why were Summer's eyes getting so big? Was she scared?

Don't be scared.

When people were scared, they *ran away.*

The tsunami wave must have shattered his great glass shadow. Its fragments swirled low in his middle now, throwing back reflections of his broken, shadowy self. Only sometimes those shards caught the light wrong and that self didn't look like an adult. It looked like a black-haired baby screaming, *Mommy!*

How long did a baby cry for his mother when she left him, before he gave up and decided monsters must have eaten her?

No monsters had eaten his mother. She'd just decided his father's world was too tough for her, so she'd gone back to the Pacific island home she loved and not bothered to take Luc with her.

As if maybe *Luc* was really what was too tough for her.

Oh, fuck.

Oh, shit, why was that stuff coming up again? As soon as Summer got pregnant, everything about him was supposed to turn *right.* Be healed. Be strong and secure and...oh, shit.

"Are you happy?" He made himself smile at her when he asked it, so that she wouldn't know that, right when she needed an adult male in her life, her own husband had remembered that he was still a screwed-up kid.

"Of course I am!" Summer dropped her hands from his shoulders to press against her flat belly, blinking out the dark reflection of him just for a second before she opened her eyes again and turned her smile up to full voltage. That beautiful shield of a smile. Luminously gorgeous. His wife was quite literally the most beautiful woman he had ever seen. The world thought so, too, and nipped and bit at her for it, wanting to rip pieces off her to make her less beautiful, like a pack of rabid dogs. "Of course. Isn't this what we wanted?"

Oh, God, he wanted it so damn bad. He wanted to walk hand in hand in lavender fields behind four gamboling children with delicate features and black hair, everything in their lives as secure and happy as an afternoon in a hammock by a lagoon. He wanted it so badly he could *taste* it.

But to get to it, he first had to get through the part where she could run away. *Not all women run away from motherhood. Stop it, you idiot. Stop it.*

His heart beat too hard. He felt dizzy, and he had to keep pressing his forearms into the stone wall to keep from slumping his head against it.

"Really." He looked down between them at her belly but didn't dare touch it. He could touch anything. He could hold his palm down on a hot pan, as his foster father had forcibly taught him, he could handle molten sugar, he could place an exquisitely fragile net of air and sugar on a dessert and never break a thing. Hell, he'd touched Summer's body every possible place a man's hands could touch. But all the sudden, he couldn't touch her belly. "Are you really happy?"

"Of course I am." She smiled at him.

If only half of Summer's smiles weren't lies. He knew she couldn't help it. He knew it was her defense mechanism. And yet it would be so damn helpful if he *actually knew what she was thinking.*

"Come here." He turned to rest his back against the wall, pulling her against him as if he was the strong one, as if he was the one who could keep them secure. Not as if he was relying on a wall to hold him up. "There you go." His fingers kneaded into the base of her spine. There, just on the other side of those bones, his little baby was growing.

Don't you dare faint, bordel. That would not reassure Summer that he was strong enough to handle everything *at all.*

I am. I swear I am. You can always count on me. You won't ever need to dump me and your baby for a better life.

And if I can knead molten sugar, I can keep kneading her spine without jerking my hand away.

A man could always handle more than his body wanted him to realize.

Summer's hands slid around his waist, fighting their way between stone and his skin, holding on hard.

I've got you, he thought to her as he tried not to pass out. He stroked her spine. *I've got this.*

Her body slowly relaxed. When all her muscles were melted against him, when all her weight was his, she slowly rubbed her face against his chest in this intimate caress of herself against him. "I love you so much," she murmured.

He kissed her pale gold hair, his dizziness slowly starting to fade.

"*Soleil.*" He chose the man he wanted to be for her and not the man who hid deep inside. "We're going to be so happy." He focused on the feel of her hair under his stroking palm. On the weight of her relaxing into him. His arms tightened. He found that knot of joy inside him and breathed on it, trying to coax it to uncramp and trust the air, to let itself become a bonfire that burned out all fear. "We're going to be so, so happy."

Chapter 4

"Oh, my God!" Summer's mother exclaimed over the phone from Hong Kong. "Pregnant *already?* Honey. I told you to give him a few years with his beautiful wife first. You don't want the only thing he associates with marriage to be a fat wife who's always throwing up."

Summer sucked in her stomach. Damn. She took a deep breath, trying to relax it, but her muscles just wouldn't un-tense from that effort to keep it flat, not while her mother was on the phone.

She wished she'd had a chance to talk more to Luc. He'd acted kind of weird last night—not radiant with happiness, more like scared to death with it. And then he'd slipped out so early that morning and so quietly, as if he was afraid to wake her.

Shouldn't he have wanted to linger? So she could tell him, excitedly, *Hey, I think I'm feeling* sick*! This must be morning sickness!*

"Although I'm sure you'll be an *adorable* pregnant woman, honey. But you know, none of us look our best. Keep track of the calories when those cravings hit. There's no excuse for gaining more than twenty-five pounds, my doctor said."

Who could eat? *Everything* looked revolting today. Except possibly a Popsicle. A Popsicle might be nice. "Right now, I'm starting to feel sick a little," she mentioned tentatively, fishing. *What's it like, Maman? Can you give me any tips?*

Damn it. Why had she told her mother?

But she knew why. She'd had no one else to tell.

"Oh, good. Honestly, I know it doesn't feel that way now, but you're lucky if the nausea goes on longer than the usual couple of months. Otherwise it is *so* hard to keep the extra pounds off. Although my friend Tru was telling me her daughter found this milkshake that's the perfect amount of nutrients and calories. It's called *Perfect Mama.* Did you tell Luc yet?"

For one tiny, odd moment, Summer almost understood something about her mother. Something alien and a little sad, that Mai Corey would assume Summer would call her first before she told her husband. Did her mother think she and her daughter were close? Or did Mai just have that emotionally distant a relationship with the husband she accompanied all over the world? "Yes. He's...thrilled, of course." Summer kneaded her belly.

Her mother laughed. "Your father was terrible. I mean, he was very proud to be a father, of course, especially when he thought you were going to be a boy, but oh, my goodness, he couldn't stand the morning sickness and the big belly getting in his way when he wanted to—well, you know. Never mind. I'm sure you don't want a picture." Her mother laughed again.

No, Summer didn't. She really didn't. And it had nothing and everything to do with her sudden image of her father's impatience with his wife's fat belly when he wanted to have sex. "Don't tell Dad."

"Oh, no, of course not, honey! Not until after three months. There's no point, you know. Until you pass three months, the odds of the pregnancy failing are so high."

Summer's breath left her as if she'd just been punched in the stomach. Right in the womb, while she stared from the terrace of their house down to the Mediterranean.

She wanted her island. To curl up at the feet of a comfortable *mamie,* help her braid leis while she held one end steady in the grip of her toes, tell her all her worries and listen to tips and stories about babies and pregnancies and eat green mangoes—

Oh, that would be good right now—a green mango. That crisp apple-like consistency but the flavor all its own.

Oh. That would be so good, it was all she could do not to hop straight on a plane in pursuit of some. And maybe curl up in all those scents of tiare and jasmine and take a few days to sink into a world of normalcy and reassurance. A *lot* of pregnancies failed the first three months?

"I—I didn't know that." She'd thought it was a done deal. She was pregnant. They were going to have a baby. She needed to find some YouTube videos that would teach her how to change a diaper.

"I had one before you." Summer blinked at this news. "Just don't count on anything too much, all right, honey? And I won't tell your father yet. Oh, he's coming. Listen, I love you, sweetheart. Let me know once you're sure!"

I was sure, Summer thought as the lights on her phone faded at the ended call. *Just for a minute there, in the doctor's office, before I tried to tell anyone, I was so damn sure.*

Chapter 5

66 Everything all right?" Antoine asked Luc about ten minutes after the sous-chef got in that morning.

Luc glanced up from his work barely long enough to nod at his *second*. He'd done his best to find a replacement for his long-term sous-chef Patrick when he opened LEROI in the south of France. Trim, compact, brown-haired Antoine was a good guy, and did good work, was a careful mentor to their hires, did really all the things an excellent sous-chef should do. And right now, all the sudden, Luc viciously hated him.

For not being Patrick. His *real* right-hand man, who had worked beside him for twelve years, whom Luc had practically raised from the age of fifteen, who had been, in so many ways that had nothing to do with the tiny overlap of their foster home experience, his damn *brother*. He needed Patrick. The flippancy, the humor, the way Patrick would be needling him right now until he got Luc to laugh or crack or even let slip, discreetly, this tiny venting of what was actually wrong. *Everything bright and beautiful always leaves me, damn it.* Luc slammed the mass of chocolate against the counter, breaking it inside its bag.

"It's fine," he said briefly. And then: "Why?" Begging his *second* with that one word to be Patrick, to not let it drop, to poke and prod with wicked humor until Luc could let what was wrong escape out of him. Until he could understand that wrongness. Master it.

"Well." Antoine eyed the sketches, new molds, and chocolate around his chef. "You must have gotten in here at 5:30 in the morning."

Yes. Slipping out of bed in the dark. Summer had murmured, her hand catching at him, but it was better this way. What if pregnancy changed her rhythms and for once in her life, she got out of bed first in the morning and left *him*?

And he turned into a bawling mess right there, dropping to his knees, clutching her legs, begging her not to leave him?

While she tried delicately to free herself because she needed to go pee.

Yeah.

No.

No, it was better he come in here and work than become that man. He had that man hidden. He had that man compressed down inside him so tiny he'd gotten as close as the universe would allow to undoing matter's existence. And just because the pressurized containment made that man—that *boy*, that stupid *boy*—seem such dense, intense matter determined to explode outward again right now didn't mean he had to yield to it. He could keep control.

He pulled his phone out of his pocket and went to his favorites. He only had five: the restaurant line, Antoine's cell, his chef de cuisine Nicolas's cell, Summer, and Patrick. And then, in the regular contacts, all the dozens of suppliers he had to call every single time a delivery went wrong. For the whole restaurant. It had been rare, at the hotel, that he had to correct a supply issue himself. So rare that up in Paris when Luc himself took the phone, about five words, cool and cutting, were all it took to resolve an issue.

Here he had to call suppliers all the time. It seemed as if half the deliveries a day went wrong, and he'd never even had to think about the savory side of supplies before this. Damn it, Gabriel Delange, the pastry chef for whom he had once been sous, long ago, had become a restaurant owner down here—a three-star executive head chef with a pastry background, something no chef de cuisine wanted to admit was possible at the time. So Luc could, too.

Anything anyone else could do, Luc could do better. If he set his mind to it. He just had to set his mind *hard enough*. Not get distracted and not let anything drop, no matter how many fragile things he juggled in the air. So he had twice as many fragile sugar balls to juggle these days than he ever had before—he was *Luc Leroi,* damn it. He could handle anything.

He stared at Patrick's name a minute. But what was he supposed to say? *Hey, I've got some terrifying, fascinating, utterly enticing news? Also, I think you might be getting a little godson or goddaughter soon.* That sounded almost like something a normal man would say.

Or: *Look, I know you ditched me and went on to live your own life, but what the fuck am I supposed to do? I can't figure out how this is funny. I need you to tell me, so I can laugh.*

Because Patrick was so damn good at that. Luc would be getting all intense, because he was always intense, and Patrick would say something wicked, and suddenly the *light* of the situation shone through so brightly even Luc could see it and laugh and relax.

We're pregnant. Come hand me a paper bag and push my head down between my knees and make fun of me for being such an idiot, so I feel sane again.

No. He couldn't text that. Because he was *Luc Leroi.* He could handle everything himself. And because Luc had practically raised Patrick, and still Patrick had found better things in life than his old chef.

And that was *normal. Merde*, let Patrick have his wings and not be tethered by some co-dependent chef/foster brother who didn't know how to laugh at himself. Fathers had to be able to laugh, didn't they? They had to be able to let people go.

Oh, fuck, no. No, I don't want to have to let anyone else go out of my life. Please, please, please let me lock them up in a box and keep them forever.

Luc shoved his phone back in his pocket and stared at the burst of desperate creativity all around him on the marble counter. Maybe Summer could come in for lunch today and he could feed her.

He could prove to her: *I can feed you both. You'll never go hungry with me. You'll never need to dump us for an easier life. I can take care of both of you.*

It was ridiculous, given how much money Summer had and how unlikely it was that her ability to find sustenance would ever affect her choices. But his mind finally settled, as he focused on the special something he was going to make for her today. On the way her face would light as she tasted it.

He could feed her.

Yes. That would be good.

***

Distraction fractured across the steel-boned foment of creation of the kitchens. Luc smiled before he even looked around, his shoulders relaxing. Summer was here.

He glanced sideways, watching her make her way through excited apprentices eagerly offering her their latest accomplishments. She tried everything, smiled at everyone, told them how wonderful they were. Hey, Antoine wasn't an apprentice, he was Luc's own damn sous-chef, trying to impress Luc's wife. Why the hell did all his sous-chefs start flirting with his wife? The one skill Patrick had had that Luc *didn't* want Antoine to channel.

Summer smiled at Antoine, too, of course, and Luc barely managed not to shout at all of them: *Damn it! Don't fill her up! She's* mine *to feed!* Stupid, since everything his apprentices and cooks were making had come from his head. Or, fine, sometimes from the head of Nicolas Delesvaux, the chef de cuisine he had hired for the savory side. She liked Nico.

21

Sometimes the fact that she liked Nico made Luc want to stab him.

What are you trying to prove? That you can take care of her or that she'd starve without you? Let your chefs feed her.

Watch her smile for them. They were currently providing internship opportunities to two teenagers from Côte d'Ivoire, in a program Summer had helped her cousins Jaime and Cade Corey develop. It had been via Summer that Jaime got Luc involved—Summer's eyes glowing with complete trust in Luc's ability to help as she told him what Jaime had told her, about how few Ivoirian farmers had ever tasted chocolate or even knew what the cacao beans they spent their lives harvesting were for. Luc, Sylvain, Dom, and multiple other top chefs were now training a new generation who could produce chocolate—value-added product—in their own country.

Both the interns had come from exploitive labor situations in their childhood, with almost no schooling, and every afternoon, Luc let them off early so Summer could sit with them on the restaurant terrace and work on reading and math skills and how to set up their own chocolate business one day. The two teenagers adored her. They loved it when they offered her something they had made and she exclaimed in delight as she tasted it.

The kids needed this. He could share.

He could.

He *could*, he ordered himself, a whiplash of internal command.

"Hi, Gorgeous." Summer smiled at him, and he had to bend his head to hide this weird, vulnerable, happy feeling that always ran through him at the nickname. She'd started calling him that flippantly when they first met, her way of protecting herself with that shield of superficial flirtation, but now the way she used it made him feel...well, gorgeous.

A feeling something like a blush. Or a...a *dimple.* Something weird he couldn't possibly allow to show. But his lashes lifted to let their eyes meet and maybe it snuck out of him, that hidden, blushing dimple, because she blew him a kiss, her eyes laughing at him.

Aww, hell. He was so damn lucky.

"*Bonjour, soleil*," he said, and leaned across to kiss her, because he was working and that was the only way he could touch her without washing his hands. Damn, but he had a frustrating career. He could make so many miracles out of it, and in return, it consumed so many of his options. "Want a bite?" he asked, and realized just a second too late how exactly like his puppy-apprentices he sounded as he held out to her a raspberry meant for the dessert he was finishing.

She took it with just her lips, very carefully not brushing his fingers with them, but he cracked, and his thumb slid with the raspberry to tug at her bottom lip, to stroke her smile.

Now he would have to wash his hands, but who the hell cared?

"Mmm," she said. "I love raspberries."

This pure, erotic charge that ran through his body whenever she said *mmm*.

"I made you something," he offered, eager to hear it some more. Eager for that *mmm* to rise to a passion of appreciation, for it to tell him: *Yes, you have set my every sense on fire.*

"Ah." The oddest flicker on her face that made him hesitate just a second, searching her eyes, but she smiled at him and sank down onto the stool he kept in his kitchens for one purpose only: in case Summer showed up and giving her a place to sit would encourage her to hang out watching him longer. It got the hell in the way, that stool, but he kept it, just the same. "Something special?" Her smile was so delighted, so loving.

"Of course," he said, offended. What did she expect him to offer her, a cookie?

Her smile deepened into something true, affectionate and amused.

Which would make her previous smile...hold on. Was she faking her smiles with him again?

Damn it, he hated it when she did that.

How the hell am I supposed to know what's wrong and fix it when you do that to me?

And God. *What was wrong?*

His gaze flicked to her belly. And then he shifted away from it in a blur of movement, righting every single thing in those kitchens that could possibly be wrong, making *everything* perfect, down to the last hair-fine line of the way a plate was patterned or a strand of sugar was posed. *I can get it all right, Summer. Just—give me time to practice. Please?*

God, he was going to be such a shitty father.

No, don't think that. You can do anything you set your mind to.

But images flashed through him now, as he worked, not his idealistic father self strolling through lavender fields while his kids played adorably and his wife laughed with happiness and beamed at him as if he had hung the sun, but the fathers he had actually known. The father who had dragged him through streets and Métros begging for change, the foster father who had never smiled at him, just nodded once in firm approval if he practiced something ten thousand times and got it right, and *merde*, Summer's father, that son of a bitch. The man who made someone as beautiful and perfect as *her* believe she was crap.

He came back to her with his special gift for her today. Not a cage, no, of course not. He'd already made her several variations of cages out of chocolate, all lined with gold and tempting things inside. It had been his perhaps misguided notion of courtship, back when they first met. He was trying to get over that. *I protect you, not cage you. The bars of chocolate are to keep you safe. I*

24

hold you in my hand to nurture you, to hold you up. Not to crush you into a tiny ball so I can keep you.

Well, damn it, he was *working* on it.

So today he had made a well of chocolate like the bell of a tulip and filled its gentle, protective depths with a liquid mango caramel, and leading into that sticky caramel he'd placed little pomegranate seeds, rich points of red drawing the innocent prey deeper and deeper into the well, closer and closer to that caramel from which there was no escape.

He stared at the dessert a moment as he set it on the counter between them. *Merde.* Was he still that messed up?

"Luc." Summer lifted a hand to touch his cheek, and pleasure just sank through him. It was so hard for him to touch her while he was working, but she could always touch him. He loved it so much he now knew exactly why puppies acted like such ridiculous animals when someone touched the top of their heads. "Pomegranate seeds?" Her eyes were indulgently chiding.

He glanced back at them guiltily. He'd promised to stop that.

Stop thinking of himself as the Lord of Hell who had trapped his hope of sunlight in here with him in the dark.

"Just, ah, four of them," he said, ridiculously.

Her palm settled into a full caress of his cheek. "You know, that story never talks about what Spring gave the Lord of Hell, to lure him into her world, too."

"Kisses, probably," Luc said helplessly, staring at her mouth. It was such a beautiful mouth. And he was working so damn hard. He really missed it. Not quick kisses in the kitchen, where everyone could see them, but sink-into-them-and-take-his-time, hot open kisses that went on forever, until he had all her clothes off, until he had his hand up between her thighs, until, until...

She blew him a kiss, pursing her lips so sweetly and slowly and drawing it out so long that he could feel the tiny brush of air from it across his lips.

Oh, God, I love you.

He licked his lips and had to turn away, to handle things before he lost a handle on himself.

"And you're not the Lord of Hell, Luc," she called after him, although several of his staff looked at her skeptically at that. Summer laughed and winked at them. "Not mine, anyway."

Wasn't he? Even as hard as she was finding it to adjust to being here? She still didn't think he had dragged her out of her island paradise on earth into his hell?

She still wasn't ready to quit on him and run back to where she was happy?

A vision slashed across his sub-conscious, so deep he didn't even have to acknowledge it, those fragments like a tumbling mirror shard orbiting fast and deep somewhere down there around the center of his soul: a black-haired baby being abandoned before he was old enough to sit up, a mother going off to her easier, happier life without him in the islands.

God, he wished he could clean those jagged, slashing fragments out of his soul.

She's maternal, he told his screwed-up soul. *She adores kids. She would never, ever abandon her baby.*

So that secret vision deep down in his soul changed, obligingly, entirely obedient. Now it wasn't of a black-haired woman leaving a black-haired baby for the islands, but of something so vicious and cruel he couldn't breathe: a golden-haired woman taking her black-haired baby with her and leaving the black-haired father entirely alone.

Oh, God. *Fuck you,* he told his imagination. *Fuck you to hell. I've got a happy marriage, with a happy wife, who is happily pregnant. Leave me the fuck alone.*

He glanced up into the mirror set high on one wall to allow him to keep an eye on the pass from the far side of the kitchen.

And saw Summer quickly dig her spoon under the dessert and scrape the entire thing into the trash, grabbing scraps from Antoine to cover it up so he wouldn't see it.

When he turned around, she was sucking on her spoon as if she'd just devoured the whole thing and was lingering over the last bite, smiling at him as if everything in her life was delicious.

And that smile was a lie.

Chapter 6

Thank God Luc hadn't caught her, Summer thought, installing herself behind his desk in his office. Throwing one of his desserts away, holy crap. His brain might have exploded. Or, worse, his heart.

She pressed her hand to her belly as if she could squoosh out queasiness. *You've got to get along with me, kid. You've got a very sensitive father.*

She wiggled the mouse and Luc's computer screen came alive. With his accounting program open.

Oh, crap.

Why did he do that to her? Did he not trust her with his freaking accounts, or what was it? Granted, she didn't have an accountant's training, but she'd gotten a summa cum laude in economics at Harvard, had funded multiple start-ups whose success following her business plans had grown her portfolio into the tens of millions, and was the daughter of one of the richest self-made investors on the planet. So she was a little more comfortable with the ins and outs of money than Luc was.

He always made such a mess of the accounts when he attacked them.

He was kind of adorable, actually, with how frustrated he got. He'd be a lot more adorable if he'd just relax and *trust her* to take control of this, but she'd known she was marrying a control freak before she took her vows.

So she sighed and shook her head, smiling just a little. Then set about straightening the mess out. If she didn't pour herself into the restaurant for Luc...well, it wasn't as if she had anything else to do with her time here but paint her nails. She tutored the apprentices Jaime sent, but all the local schools had kept their doors closed firmly in her face. No certification to teach in France and a bad reputation as a media-hungry socialite to go with it.

Accounts straightened, she set up a password access to the files with the login name "CallYourWife" and the password "kisses".

Okay, fine, she was sappy. But it made Luc smile, things like that. It relaxed, for just a minute, all the tension he accumulated in him in a day in the restaurant.

Summer flexed her shoulders and looked at the time. Lunch was approaching. She went out onto the floor to help prep the tables.

She'd get a chance to talk to Luc eventually today. No point interrupting his work just so he could help her recover from a conversation with her mother. No point sharing that worry about something going wrong at all, actually.

It would be fine.

She could handle this. A smile broke out on her face all at once, and she touched her belly as she realized that, for the first time in her life, *Someone is really counting on me.*

Chapter 7

L uc worked late. He had to. They were swamped, and the new team couldn't handle a damn thing without him, and there had been an issue with the grease trap. The grease trap. At the Hôtel de Leucé, they didn't have problems with grease traps. People made sure problems like that stayed out of their top chef's way.

He worked late, proving he could do this. Proving his desserts were irresistible, trying not to think about Summer's face as she scraped hers off into the trash.

The trash.

All the time he'd pursued her in Paris, all the desserts she had refused, she'd *never* gone so far as to throw one in the trash.

Let's not think about it.

Anyway, *merde*, he didn't have any time to waste now, to make this restaurant famous. Hell, he was still dependent on his multibillion-dollar heiress wife to wait tables and do accounts to help get the place going. He had to get his act together.

He had a baby on the way. He couldn't slack off and go home early *now*.

So he was surprised to find Summer still awake when he got home, in bed with her laptop on her knees.

She slapped it closed it as soon as she saw him— and smiled.

His heart started to beat too fast. Why was she smiling at him like that? He'd thought they'd gotten over that. The fake smile.

The way they'd gotten over his pomegranate seeds.

The pomegranate seeds she hadn't eaten.

Will you stop!! he told his damn imagination.

"What are you looking at? Baby names?" he asked
hopefully as he undressed. Which, fine, he *did* do in the
bedroom instead of the bathroom just so she would
watch him. He *loved* it when she was still awake when
he got home and watched him. It made all his muscles
feel—*alive.*

He loved when she got up and came to him right
away and pressed her face into his throat with a little
humming sound as she breathed in his scent. *Mmm, let
me guess. What were you working on today?*

It flattened him out, when she didn't. Left him feeling
deflated and—wistful. Like tonight. Tonight she just
shook her head, kneading her belly. "We should wait to
think of names."

They should? His stomach tightened. Why would
they want to put off thinking of names? Wasn't that just
a way of imagining their lives together? Imagining a boy,
imagining a girl, imagining themselves calling someone's
name and that little someone looking straight to them as
if they were that little someone's world?

"I just made sandwiches," she said apologetically. "I
didn't feel up to cooking."

It still squeezed his heart with this strange, intense
joy that she fed him. Nobody ever fed *him.* "Sandwiches
are perfect."

She smiled at him as if he'd somehow said
something precious and reached out a hand. When he
took it, she carried his to her lips and kissed the inside
of his fingers. "You're so far the opposite of spoiled," she
said caressingly.

It just melted his heart out when she did things like
that to him. Every single time. His fingers tingled where
she had kissed them, and the tingles darted out in weird
little zigzags through his body, as if his nerves had never
grown proper pathways for that kind of message to his
brain.

"I don't spoil you nearly as much as I would like to,"
he breathed, bending over her. Ah, that scent—that

sweet, tropical scent of her as if he could stretch out in the shade of a palm tree with her and while away a long summer evening in the sand. His mouth sought hers. The kiss deepened until he had forgotten all about the sandwiches or any other hunger but this. He lifted his head to study the lips he had turned so lush and soft.

"You know what would be really good right now?" those lips asked wistfully. "A Popsicle."

Luc blinked. "You want me to make you a Popsicle?" Damn, he'd known they should have installed a blast chiller in their home kitchen. How did amateur cooks even stand it, not to have one? He didn't even have a can of liquid nitrogen on hand here. The things were so damn dangerous if an amateur mishandled them.

Definitely not something to have in a house with a small child.

"Or raspberries," Summer said, her tone wrapping the word up with such craving it sent an eroticized charge all over his skin. "Raspberries would be nice."

Really? Some beautiful great flats of them had been delivered this afternoon at the restaurant, thanks to his early-morning strangling of his supplier the day before. What had he been thinking not to bring some home? "I can go get you some."

Yes! Let me feed you. He was starving himself, but he was already imagining how he would arrange the raspberries, maybe a heart because she loved sappy little things like that, and—

She shook her head, slipping out of bed. "Don't be silly." She touched his chest, and his whole body perked up in anticipation of her nose nuzzling into his throat, of that *mmm*. But she just went into the bathroom. "I'd be asleep by the time you got back."

Oh.

As the water ran behind the closed door, he looked at her laptop. Then sideways at the bathroom door.

He'd never, ever invaded her privacy this way before. But then, well—she'd never actually slapped her laptop closed when he came into the room with guilty haste before either.

What was she looking at, mommy porn?

He'd gathered vague impressions of women's sex drives changing while they were pregnant—mostly from unmarried line cooks who liked to fantasize out loud while they were working, so he wasn't sure how accurate his information was. Still, just because Summer might be embarrassed by some little new fantasy she was having didn't mean *he* would be. In fact, he'd kind of like to be prepared to surprise her with the satisfaction of it.

Maybe tonight. While it was fresh in her mind.

Refusing to acknowledge any other possible reason for invading her privacy, he opened the laptop enough to peek at her screen.

MISCARRIAGE said the main tab, and the blast of it froze him to the marrow. He slammed the screen closed. *What?*

He knocked on the bathroom door. "Summer? Are you okay?"

"I'll be out in a minute!" she called, her voice strained.

"Is everything all right? Do you feel all right?"

"*No!*" she snapped. "Luc, go away!"

And then ragged, horrible sounds.

He shoved the door open, and Summer was crouched over the toilet, body wrenching miserably.

Oh, fuck. He landed beside her on his knees, wrapping his arms around her. "Summer. Summer."

"Luc, go *away*," she wailed, and had to gag again. "Don't look at me like this," she said miserably, sagging against his arms and the toilet seat, turning her face away as she tried to wipe it.

"Shh," he said, stroking the back of her neck, twisting her hair out of the way. This he could do. Hold her, no matter what went wrong. He could do that. "Is something wrong? Should I call 112?" *Is this a miscarriage?* Oh, fuck.

"I just stood up too fast, I think," she said, still trying to hide her face from him. She flushed the toilet and closed the lid, trying to shut it all away. "I think this is what people call morning sickness."

"It's the middle of the night!"

"My mother said it could be any time of the day."

"You asked your mother for advice?" Hell. That couldn't be good.

She looked up at him miserably, still pale and damp from the bout of vomiting. "I don't have anyone else to ask, Luc."

They'd only been here three months. And Summer had always had a hard time making female friends. His heart twisted. Except on that island. She was surrounded by friends on that island.

"We'll get some books." He lifted Summer up in his arms as he stood and carried her the two feet to the sink, then supported her as she washed her face. "You're all right, aren't you? You feel"—he touched her belly delicately, all he could bring himself to do, as if he, who could handle the most fragile filament of spun sugar without breaking it, might suddenly do clumsy harm— "all right?"

This breakable sensation to his happiness was waking up every crazy part of him.

She bumped him back from her. "Will you go away and let me brush my teeth?" she said, embarrassed.

Well, he could understand why she would be embarrassed. He kissed her nape. "I love you," he whispered and left her to it.

That kind of put paid to the mommy porn fantasies, he thought, as he settled back onto his side of the bed. Still, he was glad he'd been able to help. He had helped a little bit, right? Even though it was her body that had wrenched helplessly. Even though he had knelt there perfectly fine, while she suffered. Even though she'd pushed him away.

Shit, he wished he could have helped.

He closed his eyes. Focusing on the nape of her neck as he had kissed it. Worrying about her worry about miscarriages. Trying not to think about that second tab, the one she hadn't been looking at when he came in but which had been looked at some time and still lurked there on her screen, a click away—an airline ticketing service.

Chapter 8

Summer looked at the baby swing doubtfully. It would be nice to have someone to debate this with. Not Luc, obviously. He was too busy working. His only day off, Sunday, the stores here were closed, so baby shopping was clearly going to be a solo deal.

Maybe her phone? She could imagine the conversation without even pulling it out.

So this one has the Consumer Report *rating, but some reviewers on Amazon said its motor quit after two weeks.*

Phone: *I'm not sure I understand.*

And this other one looks really cute, and it has that side to side swing motion that some reviewers said was good, but it's all pastels, and I thought I read babies could only really see black and red.

Phone: *I found fifteen places matching swing dance clubs. Thirteen are fairly close to you.*

Look, money is no freaking object, can I just have a swing that is perfect for my baby?

Phone: *Here's what I found on the web: "How to Perform the Perfect Golf Swing".*

You are a terrible substitute for human companionship.

Phone: *OK, I found this on the web: Human beings are innately social and are shaped by their experiences with others (en.wikipedia.org).*

Damn phone. She shoved it into her back pocket where it had a high chance of ending up in the washing machine.

Maybe she could fund some start-up that could design baby things that were genuinely perfect.

Hey. Wait a minute. That might actually be a good idea. She could find a couple of MIT grad students who were eager to make their mark on the world and had enough self-confidence to not feel threatened by Summer just because her father had so much money he could buy off God. They might even *like* her because she was the source of their funding, and she would be able to *talk* to them and bend over tables with designs and lay out plans.

What if it was something like working with Cade and Jaime Corey on Jaime's project to bring young people up from cacao-growing regions to learn the other end of chocolate production? That had been *fun*. Cade and Jaime had *brains*, and they acted as if it was okay for Summer to use hers, too. If she opened her mouth, they didn't give her that look women usually did, as if they wanted to claw her skin off, starting with her face.

Maybe she'd been moving in the wrong social circles, before her island. Maybe she could find some more brilliant, go-getting women who didn't have time to bother with jealousy. Or knew her as someone other than an infamous, attention-hungry socialite.

And she might have some people she could talk to, that way.

Not be here trying to figure out how to get raising her baby right entirely alone.

She tried the mobile on the red and black one and winced. Surely a mobile should play actual music instead of electric sounds?

Darn it. How could a simple swing be so complicated? She wandered away from them, through the frightening array of things she probably needed to correctly select for her baby. What did that *do*? The blue thing to help them sit up—was that really necessary? Was that even good for them? And these sling things— they didn't suffocate the baby? How did you wear them?

She was damn sure no one had ever worn *her* close and warm in a sling as if she was too precious to be left alone.

37

(Even Luc, these days, didn't seem to have any trouble leaving her alone.)

(Shut up. He's just working. Find something worthwhile to do yourself and quit whining.)

She put three different slings in her basket. Surely one of them would work. And whether her baby was loved—that was one problem she could solve. She would do all the loving that baby could possibly need.

She stopped at a table of carefully folded onesies. *Potion du bonheur,* the little pale purple one said. *Happiness Potion.* She touched it, cautiously. So soft and so tiny. Aww, there was a little pink one that said, *Princesse de la Joie.* She probably couldn't get her children anything that said princess on it. People would hate them enough already just because they were hers.

But still...she stroked the word *joie.* Joy.

Tears welled up in her eyes out of the blue, a sneak attack of weakness that just hit her from all the sides where no one stood to share this moment with her, from the back that no one protected, from the side where no one's shoulder brushed warm and strong against hers. From up a little, at an angle, where she couldn't glance to share this fragile, scared, she'll-be-that-little joy.

She left the store quickly, striding down yellow, angled streets of old Nice to the Promenade des Anglais. She walked along it end to end, blue sea to the left, old, elegant hotels to the right, topless bathers trying to sun on the gray pebble beach, casual tourists and elegant Niçois brushing past her on the walk. When she was incognito, she loved women's jogging outfits in Nice: the long free hair, perfectly brushed, sliding sexily along shoulders with every little jog, the make-up, the earrings, the elegant shoes that could not possibly be good jogging wear, but hey, they looked classy. When she was recognizable, she knew she was expected to dress like that, too.

But she had on sunglasses and a baseball cap on her head from a small Midwest college, and among all the tourists in Nice, she should be fine. Plus, she'd been out of tabloid circulation for four years, and even though she'd made a splashy comeback, with all those public disputes with Luc when she first showed up again, surely photos of her looking drugged or ridiculous or upset weren't worth anything like what they used to be. So she tried to relax, playing guessing games as to which of the joggers were French and which tourists or students abroad from America.

Probably she shouldn't be shopping for things for the baby yet anyway. The thought fought its way under the guard of that too-easy guessing game. Probably she was all alone because she was the only one who believed in this baby yet. *Luc can't prioritize a baby who might not even make it the first trimester over his restaurant. The restaurant is his* life.

She covered her belly with her hand, and then descended from the walk onto the ankle-turning pebbles, sitting on a bank of them to stare out at the Mediterranean.

God, she missed her southern sea. Her volcanic sand beaches. Her mango tree behind her house and the tiare bush by the corner, the jasmine growing up her concrete wall. Her people.

People.

Any people at all.

She picked up one of the rounded *galets*, the big gray pebbles, and rubbed it between her fingers, then tossed it into the calm sea. She'd lived on a lagoon, so the flatness of the sea wasn't *that* different. And the salt smell was more or less the same, if you could filter out the exhaust fumes. You could kind of pretend.

You could pretend all kinds of things, really.

That you didn't need anybody and were just fine on your own. That everything was going to be all right. That you were a strong person. That you could be a good mommy.

She'd always been really good at pretending herself right into the moments when none of it came true.

She sighed and leaned her head back, staring at the sky. *Oh, shut up, Summer. Buck up and handle the choice you made and above all take care of this baby.*

Her mouth softened, and her hand snuck back over her belly, caressing it, as a little light filled her, this strange light that was so soft and yet so powerful it seemed to reach to the bright blue sky above where the gulls flew. *My baby. Mine.*

I'm going to get this right, kid. I promise.

She sure missed having someone to talk to, though. She wondered how much trouble her tummy would have with a trip to the island.

Chapter 9

Every time Luc glanced at Summer, she was sucking so eagerly on the mango ice pop Luc had made her that a man had to be grateful the length of his chef's jacket hid his reaction to that eager mouth.

And yet somehow, the drips on the marble counter below it grew and grew, until he turned back from some issue to catch her swiping one of his sous-chef's towels to clean it up, the tip of the ice popping right back into her mouth when he looked at her, as she made an eager *yum* sound. She was letting it melt whenever his back was turned. And *pretending* to like it.

Damn it, he was never trusting her when they had sex again. He was going to keep his fingers right where he would *know* she wasn't faking anything.

He drew a breath and let it slowly out. "What flavor did you want?" he asked, not between his teeth at all. "For your ice pop?"

"Lime," she said wistfully. And quickly, "But this is wonderful. You know I love mangoes. It's so sweet of you to make my favorite."

And she didn't, last time he had checked, particularly like lime. "I'll make you some lime."

"You know what would be delicious?" she asked longingly.

No, but his whole body pricked awake, ready to give it. *Aroused* to give it.

"Pickles."

His whole body felt as if it had just taken one to the groin. "*Pickles?*"

She nodded eagerly.

His shoulders slumped. He shifted into his chef de cuisine's side of the kitchens and sent the first *commis* he encountered running for some of Nicolas's pickles. Not jealous in the *least* that his chef de cuisine got to feed her and not him.

No. Because jealousy like that would be crazy.

His chef de cuisine, Nico, who was all about living from the land and using all nature's resources, had pickled watermelon rinds, pickled pears, pickled peppers, pickled beets, pickled figs, and pickled corn. Probably gleaned from local fields post harvest. The man liked to stroll through farmers' land, picking up all the leftovers that would otherwise rot. Luc would probably get arrested if he ever tried that kind of thing—not to mention that his whole childhood flinched inside him in desperate panic when he even thought about it—but somehow people let Nicolas do anything.

Summer picked at every single type of pickle, biting her lip in a clear battle with revulsion. Kind of nice to know he wasn't the only man failing her right now.

Except—shit. He had to manage to feed her. He had to.

Summer tried a watermelon rind and sagged a little, pushing it away. "Just *regular* pickles," she said. "Like—" She glanced around to make sure Nicolas wasn't in earshot and lowered her voice so even Luc could barely pick it up. "From the store."

It was a good thing he could count on Summer's manners in all situations. If she'd said that loudly enough for Nico to hear it, he might be hiring a new chef right now.

Unfortunately, he couldn't hire a new self, no matter how hard he tried; he could only deal with the self he had. The insane self that kept trying to get out of its padded cell.

He slipped one of his apprentices some money. "Enzo. Run down to the *épicerie* and get me a jar of pickles, all right? Don't let Nicolas see."

But when he slid Summer a tiny bowl of the miniature *cornichons* Enzo brought, she took one bite and grimaced, visibly trying to control a gag. "American pickles," she said, shoving the *cornichons* as far away from her as she could. "You know, with dill?"

Luc went and found Nicolas, breaking it as gently as he could that Summer had refused every single one of his special pickles and only wanted this dill stuff. Nico took it oddly well. He even seemed amused. Sometimes the guy was disconcertingly rough-and-ready, take-it-as-they-come, compared to Paris chefs. "Sure, I can make them. But, Luc," the burly, brown-haired farmer of a chef said with that kind of callused-hand gentleness of his, as if he was taking care of a newborn lamb, "they take several weeks."

Luc stared at him. He knew that. He'd never actually made a pickle, but he'd been working in kitchens all his life. He did know that. He just...went out onto the tiny terrace of the restaurant. Pacing between pots of lavender, he called Sylvain Marquis, a top chocolatier in Paris who had been sufficiently confused about his priorities in life to marry the heir to and vice president of the world's largest producer of mass market crap, otherwise known as Corey Chocolate. Cade Corey Marquis, Summer's second cousin. "I need to talk to Cade."

"Sorry," the chocolatier said cheerfully. "She's only allowed to talk to handsome chefs by prior appointment between 3:14 and 3:15 in the afternoon. What is it? Is it about one of the apprentices? How are they working out for you anyway?"

"Fine," Luc said blankly.

"Are Cade and Jaime sending you the easy ones?" Sylvain asked suspiciously. "Because a couple of the kids I've gotten..." He let his voice trail off in a way that spoke volumes.

"They don't act that differently than some of my foster brothers." Luc shrugged. Or sometimes that differently than he himself had once acted. Sylvain came from a happy family, that was his problem. Or rather his lack of a problem. Luc, on the other hand, just trained whatever kids he got and dealt with whatever he had to deal with. And Summer mothered them and patiently taught them letters when they were illiterate, and as far as he could tell, the kids were as happy as bees in honey. They still needed to relax and accept no one was threatening the honey, but from Luc's personal experience, that might take years.

Decades.

A lifetime, at the rate he himself was going.

A vision of Summer's face, the patience and warmth as she sat there with those kids.

He grabbed the image and fed it to the insane him he was keeping locked in a padded cell. *She's maternal, you fucked-up idiot. She* loves *kids. She would never, ever run out on her baby.*

What do you know? Insane Him asked. *Maybe your mother was maternal, too. Before she had you. And then you were so damned difficult, you ruined that for her.*

He slammed the cell door back on the bastard.

"Listen, is Cade there? I have an American question." Maybe he should have called Jaime. She and Dom had been together for over a year now, and Dom was starting to act mildly sane about her. It gave a man hope for his own case.

Sylvain laughed. "All right, but you only get one minute. I'm timing you!"

"Ignore him," Cade said as she came on the phone. "It's the only thing to do. What do you need?"

"Pickles," Luc said.

A tiny silence on the other end of the connection. Possibly a choked sound. "Pickles?"

"Whatever kind of American pickles that you and Jaime and Summer would have been eating as kids, I assume. Can't you eat normal pickles like the rest of us?"

More amusement on the other end. "Well, one person's idea of normal, Luc, is another person's crazy."

When they were talking about food, he was pretty sure the French got to decide what was good and what was crazy. For God's sake, her country had invented peanut butter! And then put it with chocolate! But he needed a favor, so he resisted rubbing it in. She got touchy about those ghastly Corey products sometimes. "Whatever you consider normal pickles. I think that's what I need." And, realizing that required some explanation: "Summer's pregnant."

At the startled gasp and then the squeal of excitement, he suddenly realized he should have let Summer break that news. "No way!" Cade was exclaiming. "Is she really? That was fast! You guys just got married! Oh, man, wait until I tell Jamie! When's it due? Is it a boy or a girl? Do you need a—"

Luc held the phone away from his ear and stared at it. Cade knew how to squeal? Cade Corey? Damn, he really should have let Summer be the one to receive that first burst of delighted enthusiasm from her cousin. Shit, he just hadn't realized. The news had hit *him* with terror. "I need pickles," he said firmly. "American pickles. With dill."

"There's an American store here in Paris," Cade said. "Can I overnight them or do you want a courier to bring them down today?"

Sometimes he just loved knowing so many billionaires. "Today," he said. Made for kind of expensive pickles, but he'd never had a particularly good grasp of money anyway, and ever since he'd married Summer, the excessive amounts floating around all these Coreys had completely lost him. Whatever it cost, he was pretty sure it wouldn't break anyone's bank account.

When Summer got her pickles, she *devoured* them. He nibbled one, puzzled, watching the pleasure on her face, trying to imagine what was going on in her mouth, that the crunchy burst of acid would feel so good to it. Then she threw her arms around him and kissed him to say thank you, and he tasted the vinegar on her lips and almost, for a second, knew.

45

Chapter 10

S ummer was still smiling a little bit, a jar of pickles in one hand and a plastic box of lime ice pops under one arm, when she let herself into their house up on one of those rugged, Mediterranean cliffs, where lavender and stone walls framed the garden and terrace from which she could look out over the sea. The silence of the house echoed back at her, and her smile faded before she could stop it.

She didn't want it to. She clutched at her jar of pickles and said, *No. We're fine.* But her smile defied her and wouldn't come back out. *No one's here to see. I don't have to come out if I don't want to.*

You're all alone.

She set the jar of pickles down slowly on the kitchen counter, and the little noise it made clicked all the way through the silent house. It made her skin prickle, how completely no other sound responded to it. She set down her purse, in as bustling a way as she could, turning on music. Oh, was that the right music for the baby? Was she supposed to be listening to classical music or something? She put the lime ice pops in the freezer and went online to download Beethoven's Ninth.

Then she went out on the terrace and gazed down at the twilit sea, brushing her hand back and forth across the lavender in the nearest pot to release the scent. Solitude felt more normal on the terrace than inside. Thoughtful, quiet. A choice.

Because it *was* a choice. Not an easy choice, not a walk-in-the-park choice, but a definite choice she had made. To leave her island, for Luc. To face solitude at first. To support him, while he worked like a dog to build a new restaurant, a new reputation here, and to believe in him, that he would not have to work that hard and leave her this alone forever.

To draw on all the strength and sense of self she had built in those islands to help her get through the first, toughest part until she could build strength and value here, too.

She covered her belly with her hand. *So quit whining, Summer. Grow up. Quit needing so much attention. Don't be so spoiled.*

A little hiccup of hurt in her heart at the word.

She repeated it to herself, harshly, like her dad: *Spoiled.*

Right.

She bent her head, stroking her belly. *I want to spoil you. But I'm not supposed to. Not supposed to ruin you that way. I want you to turn out—perfect. So everyone will love you.*

A ripple of profound shock, her head jerking up. That last part had sounded like her mother.

No. No, no, no. I'm not doing that to my baby. Not teaching her how to be perfect as if that's the only way she can hope to earn love.

Oh, hell, how am I supposed to get this right?

***

A light was glowing on the terrace outside their bedroom when Luc got home, the doors between bedroom and terrace wide open so that the indoor and outdoor spaces blurred. Lavender scented the space, from the pots tucked against the walls, and stone, and maybe a distant hint of the sea. Summer sat at the tall table there, her laptop open.

"You're still up?" Luc came behind her to put a hand on her nape, rubbing her silky hair as he bent to kiss her. She closed the laptop right away, though. Had that been a glimpse of a coconut palm on that web page? His stomach knotted. "Shouldn't you be getting your rest?"

Pregnant women got tired, right? He himself only rested when Summer dragged him down into a hammock, so it was hard to wrap his mind around the idea of rest as an actual need. He had made it to the age of thirty without ever having a moment's true rest, so how could it be a need? No, it was this special gift, this privilege, that Summer gave him.

"You're up late, too," she said, a tiny, rough grain of sand in the silk of her. She must be sleepy. He smiled, thinking about ways he could make her sleepier—all soft and heavy and curling up satisfied—and gave her nape another pet before he started to undress.

"Bloom," he explained as he pulled off his shirt. Discovering those should-have-been gorgeous chocolate domes covered with the pale, splotchy shades of chocolate improperly tempered, a discovery he'd made half an hour before the service started, still made him want to gnash his teeth. "That's why I'm late. On all the chocolate domes. It's our most popular dessert, Summer, and...every single one. I swear to God you have to watch this team *every single second*. Who doesn't know how to temper chocolate?"

"Me." A glimmer of a smile, just this elusive shimmer of it over his skin. God, he missed her. He knew it was bad of him to try to dominate all her time and attention that way, but he loved when she came to hang out all evening in the restaurant, helping where she could, tucking herself into a corner when things got so crazy she was in the way. It made his whole evening just kind of—*sing*.

And *God*, but she was good at handling customers. Whenever she stood in for the maître d', people acted as if they'd been suddenly invited into the private home of a princess and allowed to dine there, welcomed with that elusive friendliness of hers that seemed to say: *This is a rare and special grace for you, to dine here with us this evening. Isn't it wonderful to be so lucky? What special people you must be.*

He was pretty sure she even believed that about him, that anyone who tasted his food was blessed by the gods. "I'll teach you." Oh, yeah, what a delicious idea. Him standing behind Summer, hand around her wrist, guiding her as they lifted and spread melted chocolate over marble. As she dipped a knuckle in it to learn when the temperature was right...as she sucked it off...or offered it to him. "Whenever you want."

A tiny flicker of a glance that confused him, as if she didn't believe him, when he was already being sucked right into that fantasy so deeply that his mouth watered from it and it was all he could do not to bend over her right now and suck on far more of her than just a knuckle. He could start with a knuckle.

"You've been working late a lot," she murmured to her laptop, open again now that he was at an angle where he could no longer see it.

He paused with his hands at the waist of his pants and searched her face, but he could only see that exquisite, delicate profile, as she focused on what she was typing. "It's just getting everything started. We've only been running two months." He hesitated, feeling ridiculous and awkward, all things he had trained himself long ago not to feel and definitely not to show. But he could show them to Summer, surely. "I want to have a star for the baby," he admitted, trying not to flush. He shrugged his shoulders to make them more comfortable. But he could expose this to Summer. She was the only person in the world to whom he could expose his heart in words, and not just food. "I want her daddy to have a star." The heat grew in his cheeks.

She looked up at that, and her expression softened. The warmth of it reached out to him, curling tendrils around his bare, tired body. Making it less tired. Making him want to hurry up with that shower so he could come back over to her. "You've had three already," she said gently. "Luc—she won't care about a star."

Oh, God, he hoped Summer was wrong about that. Because that was what he was *good* at, getting stars. He didn't have anything else he was sure he could get right. "She'll be proud when she's older," he tried, more tentative than he liked. She would, wouldn't she?

"Maybe," Summer said. "But an adult child's pride in her father is a small compensation for feeling loved by him when she's young."

Oh. And Summer would know, wouldn't she? He flexed his fingers into his palms and ran through all the things he used to tell himself, when he was glaring at his father-in-law, that he would do better as a father. Play with his little girl on the monkey bars, let her sit in his lap whenever she wanted, sit her on the counter while he worked so he could make her beautiful, special things just for her. He could still do all those things. He could.

And they might even work, too. They couldn't be worse than the way his and Summer's parents had raised—or abandoned raising—them. Right?

Shit, how did he get this parenting thing perfect before they had the actual baby? What was he supposed to practice on?

"It will be better by the time she—or he—is born," Luc promised. "The restaurant will be running more smoothly, and I'll be more sure I can count on Antoine and the staff when I'm not there."

She nodded understandingly and looked back at her computer. "Don't worry, I'm used to it," she murmured to her screen. "All my boyfriends were the same way."

He stopped dead in the bathroom door, the needle sliding delicate and silver right through his ribs and lodging there. She hadn't needled him that way in a long time. He'd forgotten how good she was at it. Smiling and sweet and silky, so that you kept wondering if maybe you'd stabbed *yourself* with the needle or something, since it couldn't possibly have come from her.

He walked back across the room to her, a thin sliver of steel seeming to shift in his rib muscles with every stride. "I'm not one of your boyfriends, Summer." He leaned across the table, planting his forearms on either side of her computer, dominating her space. "I'm your husband."

Something flashed in her eyes, this bitten-back thing too ugly to say, that tightened his stomach into a knot as he stared down at her. *Don't say that, Summer. Whatever you almost said about me being your husband, don't say it.*

Oh, God, what was she going to say?

"I *thought* I had one somewhere," she murmured instead to her computer, tapping it thoughtfully.

He leaned in closer and snatched a kiss—just stole it, fierce and hard and not letting her resist it. She pulled back and looked at him. And then she shook her head a little and leaned back toward him. He tried to kiss her hard again, just take her over, *I own you, you're my wife, you're* mine, and she shook her head again, twisting her mouth free and then bringing it back, softer. Gentling him. Seeking what *she* wanted.

Oh. As the softness and warmth caressed through his own possessive anger, the tension in him unwound. He could do this, too. He shifted around the table, pulling her into his arms. Tension coiled back up again at the feel of her body, but such a healthier tension, whole and hungry instead of jagged and starved. "I should take a shower," he murmured.

She licked the hollow of his throat. "You taste like salt," she whispered. "And you smell like—mmm, lime?"

He petted her back, and she snuggled more deeply into him, tightening all the muscles in his body while her own muscles softened. Oh, that was a perfect fit, his growing hardness, her growing softness. "Since when have you liked lime so much?"

"Since it smells like you," she said, and bit him. Arousal jolted through him at the tiny, hungry pressure of her teeth against his collarbone. He lifted her up into him, pulling her thighs around his hips.

Ah, yes, a perfect fit. Lovely. Lovely how this still worked. His mind flashed visions of a bump slowly getting in the way, then getting so big they had to give up this position entirely, and he stroked his hand between them over her belly, cupping it fully for the first time since she had told him, the whole awareness that a baby was in there turned surreal and beautiful. Did it feel beautiful to her? It was *happening* to her. God, how must that feel?

He kissed her again, trying to find out, trying to steal that feeling from right inside her and taste it himself. "You taste just the same," he murmured. That was strange, too, as if she should taste new and exotic. "I'm glad. I'm glad you taste like mine."

She pulled back a little, but he kept one hand firm under her butt, to keep that delicious pressure against his groin. "You don't think you'll like it when I change?"

"I think you'll be the most beautiful pregnant woman the world has ever seen," he said, in complete honesty. *Merde*, they'd probably be trying to get her to pose naked for *Vanity Fair*. And they wouldn't have to touch her up, either. She'd cause some whole new wave of Madonna paintings among artists. Probably triple next year's birth rate, with all the women who wanted to look like her.

Her face got all funny, crinkling up, her eyes so wondering it was almost as if a sheen of tears was making them sparkle. "Really?"

"Summer. How can you know so well how beautiful you are and still not *know* it?" Sometimes he hated the whole damn world that had ever gotten to her before he did.

She shrugged, all pleased and embarrassed. So he kissed one of those beautiful, strong swimmer's shoulders. She could swim much farther than he could. And yet her shoulders would always, always be so much smaller. *Is the Mediterranean enough of a swimming pool for her? Or is she missing the South Pacific?*

It was weird how that made her sound so spoiled, even in his head, when it was actually one of the least spoiled things about her. She'd spent four years in the South Pacific, on a remote island, teaching school. Shut as far away as she could from everyone in the world besides her islanders and her school kids.

Her cousin Jaime talked about how it was the only way Summer could be real. She'd warned him about it, actually, in a little moment under a coconut palm tree at their wedding, nibbling at the pork from the great roast the islanders had done for them. Not warned him away, exactly—they were already married by then—just discreetly alluded to a problem he might need to be alert to, if he took Summer away from the place she felt so real and solid to the world where she felt fragile and alone.

You're not fragile at all, he told her strong shoulder, rubbing his face against her skin, kissing his way to the curve of it. *I'm here. All around you, see? Feel how my arms have got you? And I'm only fragile for you.*

Because somehow, when I give you that fragile part of me, you give me back all my strength.

God, she felt so sweet. She smelled so sweet. She *was* so sweet. He still, to this day, could barely handle the amount of sweetness she had brought into his life, him, the world-famous pastry chef. "I love you," he whispered into her throat, up to the curve of her jaw.

Her hands climbed up his back to grip his shoulders, pulling her in tight to him. "You do?"

So much reassurance, Summer always needed. He petted her. "Of course I do," he murmured to that delicate curve of her ear. "I'll always love you."

Her arms tightened very hard around him, and she turned her face suddenly into his throat, taking a deep breath. "Even if I'm fat?"

He had a sudden vision of a plump Summer which amused the hell out of him. She was so compulsively slender. But yeah, he was pretty sure he would like it. Why not? Especially if she was comfortable with it herself.

Of course, if she ever even gained five pounds, her mother would stop by and start pinching her waist and smoothing her own clothes over her svelte form in satisfaction at being thinner than her daughter, so it wasn't like the comfortably plump Summer was ever actually going to *happen*. But—he rubbed his hands over her waist and hips. "You'd still be beautiful," he told her. "You know that, don't you?"

But she didn't. That was part of Summer's problem. She'd been so damn beautiful her whole life that she had no idea what her actual beauty *was*.

"You'll always be beautiful," he told her, kneading his hands into her butt, possibly one of his hands' top five favorite things to do in the whole world. The other four involved her body, too. "Because, Summer: You. Are. Beautiful."

As if by breaking it down into small words, she could understand.

And she did for a minute. Her head lifted, and her face lit. She kissed him, long and sweet and deep.

"But if, when you say *fat,* you're talking about being pregnant—*merde*, Summer, I've always wanted to see you pregnant out to"—he leaned her backward over his arm, which ground her hips so very nicely against his, and then backwards and backwards until there was as much room as he could imagine for a baby bump, which left her horizontal to the floor and clutching at his arms, all her security and stability dependent on him. He smiled at her, a fierce, sharp shard of joy—"here."

He'd wanted to see her pregnant so much that he'd never understood how, once he actually got it, the panic of having so much happiness to lose would reach up into his throat and *choke* him.

"Luc." Summer pulled at his arms, perturbed by her precarious position. But it wasn't precarious. It all depended on him, a tantalizing, arousing power. She could depend on him. He wouldn't let her drop.

He walked her backward toward the bed, still keeping her horizontal to the floor, laughing at her unease. *I've got you. You're mine. I won't let you fall, but you have to put yourself entirely in my hands. You're mine.*

Arousal pressed through him at the way their hips ground together with each step, at how vulnerable she was to him.

"Luc, stop," Summer said, her eyes flickering with anxiety, and he laughed and rested her on the bed.

I've got you, you know. Quit worrying. Shh, soleil. I promise you're safe with me.

But laying her back on the bed made it far too easy for her to wriggle away and escape, so he drew one hand up her arms and caught her wrists, pinning them to the bed. Oh, yes. Yes, he liked her this way, stretched out for him, his. That dark thing rose up in him, that starved, old need to ravage her, fighting for freedom from his control. *No,* he told that dark thing. He needed that control to make sure she came and came and came, to make sure every beautiful sensation in her body came from him. To keep her addicted.

"Luc," she protested, pulling at her wrists. "Let me go."

He laughed. "Use your safe word," he teased, letting his other hand trail as delicate and tantalizing as he could make it from the hollow of her throat in a little dancing pattern down her breastbone, under her breasts, down her belly.

He loved her "safe word". *Je t'aime, je t'aime, je t'aime.* She'd thrown it out there ironically once in one of the more dangerous moments of their developing relationship, when everything seemed to keep going entirely wrong. These days, it had lost all sense as a "safe word", provoking him to do more and more of whatever was making her say it and not stop, but that was okay. They were just playing. Playing that he'd captured her, playing that she couldn't break free. She liked it as much as he did. He'd know if she ever really wanted him to stop.

He felt quite sure.

"Luc, I *mean it.*" She twisted with sudden, desperate strength.

His hand hardened on her wrists in instant reaction, and she made a pleading, angry sound—and his hand jerked back as he realized what he was doing.

She scrambled away from him, while his world swirled around one hard time and stopped dead again.

Summer dove off the bed and ran toward the bathroom, slamming the door behind her.

"Summer!" He hadn't—had she felt *threatened?* He—

Then the unmistakable sounds of retching came through the door.

Oh.

His stupid, possessive games had made her throw up. All the arousal and confusion slid off him in defeated shame.

He tried to open the door and found it locked. *Damn it, Summer.* He pulled a credit card out of his wallet and wriggled it through the crack to force the lock free.

"Don't come in here!" Summer cried as he pulled the door open.

He stopped. She hadn't made it to the toilet in time and knelt with vomit in her hair and on her pretty silk pajama top. She met his eyes for one defeated second, and then flinched into herself, throwing her arms over her face and turning away, trying to hide, as she started to cry.

"Summer. *Soleil.*" He stroked her curved back. "Shh. It's all right. I'm so stupid. Shh. I'm sorry."

She shook her head, but she didn't lift it from the arms that hid it.

He grasped, dimly and distantly, that the actual morning sickness might not be his immediate fault—he'd put that morning sickness in motion a little over six weeks ago, or longer, if you counted all the times he had teased and coaxed about children and drawn visions in the air for her of how happy they were going to be as a family. But the fact that she had not made it to the toilet in time, her current agonizing shame, was most definitely due to him.

To his need to claim her. Thinking with his fucking dick.

Only it hadn't felt like just his dick at the time; it had felt more like his desperate heart.

"Shh." He drew her up by the waist, because she still kept herself as hidden as she could, and guided her to the shower, turning it on. "Shh."

"Luc, please go away," Summer said miserably.

"You know, Summer," he said very, very gently, easing the soiled pajama top up over her resistant arms, trying to make sure he didn't smear any more of the stuff on her. "You're still beautiful to me. Even right this second—*especially* right this second—you're still the most beautiful woman I've ever seen."

Her head did lift a little at that, and she stared at him over the arms that still hid most of her face, her eyes wet with tears.

"Shh." He stroked her bare spine. Then slid her pajama bottoms and sexy lace panties off with the ease of considerable practice and put her under the shower. "Summer. Sometimes I still think that when I say I love you, you have no idea what it means."

And it scared him, because it made him want to turn into a teenage boy in one of his old, disastrous, desperate relationships again, trying to *force* his love onto her, trying to *make* her understand how important it was: *I love you! You can't leave me because I love you!*

Because if she didn't know, she might give up on it too easily when things got tough and run away.

"It's not just because of this." He stretched his arm under the shower, his shirtsleeve getting soaked as he touched one of those delicate, photogenic cheekbones. He stripped his shirt off, wishing he could just strip everything off and step into that shower with her, but—

Yeah. She probably wasn't in the mood.

But she might pretend to be in the mood, because she faked things when she was insecure. Faked things just to please him, because she loved him so much that she was afraid of losing him, too. It drove him mad, because unless he managed to catch her at it, that skill at faking things made it, in fact, really hard to know when she was feeling insecure. And her insecurity was the great, giant weakness in his happiness, the thing that could bring it tumbling down.

Wasn't it? Or was that thing that always felt on the brink of tearing everything apart his own insecurity?

"It's not just because of this." He let his fingers slide with the water down her side, just brushing the curve of her breast and hip. "So if your body or your face changed, I would still love you."

Summer pressed her forearms against the shower wall, letting the water stream down over her bent head and curved back. Arousal beat in him at the view. God, he could think of *all kinds* of things to do with that view, all kinds of ways to re-assert his possession of her and make her enjoy it.

Except what kind of bastard inflicted himself on his pregnant wife minutes after she'd been throwing up and sobbing? He angled his head to better see her face. Were those shower droplets running over her cheeks or was she still crying? "You love beautiful things," she muttered to the shower. "You know you do."

"You're not a thing," he pointed out to her. She'd told him so once herself. And he'd lifted his finger to arrange a lock of her hair, just as he was doing now. Not because he thought she was a thing, but because he loved to touch her as if she was his, and he couldn't stop himself. "Remember?"

Her mouth twisted into what was at least half a smile, and she lowered her forehead to rest it on the shower wall. A sigh ran through her body.

I could make her sigh. I could make her sigh in just that position, with the water running down all over us,

58

and I'd have to hold her up because all her muscles would give up and let me take over...

Bastard. Sometimes the insane him and the him he tried to keep in control became far too hard to distinguish. Was his current hunger for her, despite and *because* of her vulnerability, a little nuts, or would every man be that much of a jerk?

Merde, what was he thinking? Half the world fantasized about his wife. Yes, every man would be that much of a jerk, if standing right here. And it didn't make him feel better about himself at all.

"I love you," he repeated out loud firmly. Because in that he did have all the other men in the world beat. He loved her more than anyone else ever possibly could.

(Although her islanders loved her, that masochistic son of a bitch he hid inside him pointed out. Loved her in a relaxed way, a sane, swing in a hammock and drink a beer and chat way. A way that made her very happy.)

Shut the fuck up before I kill you! he told that vicious little bastard.

Oh, don't you wish you could?

Summer rested her cheek against the shower wall, turning toward him at last. She smiled weakly. "Okay." After a moment, she took his hand from her back and kissed it, holding it to her face. "Okay."

He sank his shoulder against the wall beside the shower, letting his face rest against it so they were eye to eye. "*Je t'aime,*" he told her again, and her eyes drifted closed, but the corners of her mouth floated upward, and he could swear that tired smile was genuine. "Do you want me to wash your hair?"

Her eyes flew open. "Oh, God, do I have stuff in my hair?"

"A little bit," he admitted.

She grimaced, angling her head into the spray with renewed energy. "Luc, go away."

Well, at least that sounded less like a despairing, you-can't-love-me "go away" and more like a "go-away" that was secure enough again to show exasperation. He went and rinsed his day off him in a guest bathroom, then stretched out in bed, listening to the shower shut off.

He could all too easily imagine her drying off her naked body right now, all too easily imagine what he could do with a terry towel against sensitive, bare skin willingly yielded to him. But—he sighed. He supposed the whole incident had put paid to this night's mommy porn fantasies, too, hadn't it? All Luc had to think about was her trying to smile at his touch, when inside revulsion was building and building as she fought not to throw up.

Yeah.

No.

He closed his eyes. They hadn't made love since she told him she was pregnant, and he just *wanted* to. Well, he always wanted to, but the need kept growing in him to claim her again, to make sure that everything was still working all right.

But she probably wanted to stop being nauseated, too. There were all kinds of wants you didn't necessarily get when you were adapting to a pregnancy, weren't there? It was only for seven and a half more months.

A dizzying whirl of panic. *Seven and a half more months! And then they would have the actual baby.*

The hair dryer ran briefly, and then Summer came out. Was it best just to pretend to be asleep? She'd been so damned embarrassed. It still hurt his heart to see her so shamed, how deep it had cut her, as if she really, truly feared that he might not love her anymore. God.

You have to believe I love you, Summer. You have to. There's not one single other thing holding you here.

She slid into bed and snuggled right up against him, and his muscles eased. Pseudo-sleepily, he shifted so that his arm wrapped around her, settling her in. *There you go, soleil. I'm asleep so you don't have to worry about being embarrassed. But even asleep, I still love you.*

She kissed his chest. He smiled, as pleasure ran through him. She kissed it again. Ah, yes. He liked that so damn much. Another kiss, three, four...her hand stroking down from his shoulder over his—

He pressed her palm against his belly, stopping it even as all his muscles tensed. "Summer. Not tonight." *Don't fake it to try to please me. While all the time you're stamping down nausea.*

Summer stopped instantly. Then she rolled over to her side of the bed, curling up with her back to him. She must have gone to sleep immediately, probably worn out, his poor *soleil*, because she didn't move again.

Not once, in all the time he lay awake worrying.

Chapter 11

S ummer went to get a haircut. Something she had rarely worried about on her island, but she looked at herself in the mirror, the faint circles under her eyes, and thought suddenly: *Maybe Maman is right, maybe I'm letting myself go. Just a little trim to make sure the ends fall right.*

She lay with her head back against the sink as the stylist washed her hair, so tired she wanted to fall asleep right there, under the gentle wash of water and the firm massage of her scalp. The scents in the salon beat at her too strongly, and she wanted to sleep them away. Maybe when she woke up, her stomach would have stopped feeling so yucky. And then *she* would feel less yucky.

It's no big deal, she told herself. *That he pushed you away. Let's face it, vomit is not the sexiest look on any woman. Just because it shut down his sex drive for the night doesn't mean he doesn't love you anymore.*

She didn't know why she could listen to what he said, and yet sometimes there was a part of her that just didn't *hear* it. It took *forever* to sink in, as if her heart was this desperate parched earth that just could not relax enough for the rain. The rain slid off it and slid off it and finally, slowly, started to penetrate, as the earth at last loosened up and began to absorb.

I love you. I love you. I love you. Luc's voice, his dark eyes as he leaned his head against the wall by the shower and gazed into hers. She took the words out and rubbed them over and over, their resonance and the look in his eyes, like telling worry beads until the worry went away. Until her mother's voice went away. *I love you. I love you.*

It wasn't the same love at all, that deep, dark love that seemed to reach inside her and vibrate there. Not a light, caressing love that glanced over her skin, saying, *I love you, and why don't we just take care of those lines around your eyes so you look pretty? I love you, so I'm not letting you get your hopes up for a healthy baby and a happy family.*

She touched the corners of her eyes. She did have lines there, picked up young from laughing under too much tropical sun. Luc would notice a flaw much finer than one of those tiny lines on one of his desserts and throw it out, rather than associate himself with even invisible imperfection.

And the salon she was in right this second did microdermabrasion. Her mother had been pushing that since Summer came back from the islands, but Summer always looked in the mirror and thought, *There, but for a little Botox and an obsession with skin care, goes my mother.*

Still. There was nothing wrong with microdermabrasion. Just like an exfoliation, really. And her skin certainly hadn't come out better for those four years of careless tropical island living. She stroked the corners of her eyes, unable even to feel the lines her mother had pointed out, they were so fine. Her phone beeped, and she relaxed all through her. Luc.

He liked to text her photos of what he was doing from time to time, when she wasn't at the restaurant, as if he knew how much she needed the attention. Or as if he wanted to lure her over there to taste. That first possible explanation made her feel pathetic, but the second made her feel so happy.

And a third made her feel possessive and tender: that maybe he needed the attention himself. He claimed sometimes that he had a narcissistic streak, which made her laugh. She knew a lot more about narcissists than Luc did apparently. Luc most definitely wasn't one.

Why had he looked that way, about the baby? Why didn't he seem happy? She'd thought he would be overjoyed. Delirious with it. Adorable with it.

She pulled out her phone, and it was indeed a text. From her mother. *Honey, I've been looking...*

She hesitated, but—who else was she supposed to talk to about these baby things? Was she supposed to blurt it all out to the stylist, when the other woman asked her how she wanted her hair cut? "Um—like a woman who would be a good mommy and still sexy?" Yeah, right.

She touched the text to open it fully.

"Honey, I've been looking around. I know it's probably premature when you haven't even made it safe through the first trimester yet (smiley face), but you can never start too early when it comes to finding a good nanny. You want someone who knows what she's doing, because you certainly won't! (Smiley face.) The things I managed to mess up with you those first few months before I found your first nanny. You remember, the one you got fired when you snuck off that time at the Leucé? (Smiley face.) She was really good. Or Liz. Liz was amazing. You need someone like her, to make sure you raise the baby right. (Smiley face.) Anyway, Julie's daughter is about to start boarding school, and they rave about her nanny, do you want me to interview her for you? I can't wait to see you! I miss you! Love, Maman.

The stylist squeezed a great glob of conditioner into her palm, scents of vanilla and something sickening, and all at once the scents packing the salon were clamoring at Summer like starving cats, just scratching and shoving, until she lurched out of her seat and ran, her hair streaming soaked down her back, to the bathroom.

***

"I'm so sorry," Summer was still saying twenty minutes later. They'd decided to skip the cut, but Summer was paying for it anyway, and leaving a big tip, too. "I cleaned it up. I'm really sorry." She signed her name under the huge tip, and darted a glance at the stylist, who was barely controlling her revulsion. "I—I'm pregnant," she tried, in this tentative hope for—what?

Some stupid moment of solidarity or understanding, this sudden relaxation into a sisterhood of, "Oh, you poor thing, I remember when I/my sister/my friend was pregnant and she..."?

"You might want to avoid salons until you're past the worst stages, then, *madame*," the stylist said crisply, turning away with the signed credit slip in hand. "I hear the odors can be difficult."

Right. Summer slipped her card back into her purse and went out onto the sidewalk. Sometimes she wished she'd chosen to be an actress in a romantic comedy, so she could at least have someone pretend to be her chummy sidekick friend for a while.

She looked at her watch. Maybe she could just peek into the restaurant. That wouldn't be too clingy and over-dependent, would it? Maybe Luc would make her another ice pop.

A smile softened her mouth. He would definitely make her an ice pop. She just hoped she could actually eat it when it got done this time.

The restaurant's village perched above the sea—just far enough from Cannes and Nice to make the luxury crowd work for it, as Summer and Luc had put it when they found the location—and she drove back from the world of yachts and jewels and luxury salons to the world of old stone and jasmine, leaving the car at their house on a cliff above the sea and walking through the streets to the restaurant. The sound of stone under her feet, the brush of it against her fingertips, the vines and flowers climbing up old walls, and the cat that jumped from balcony to balcony as she passed, all reassured her. Even the sight of the yachts bobbing on the sea below, toward Cannes, comforted her in some way. That luxury world of yachts and judgment that she had abandoned that day she stepped off her own rented yacht, moored on the edge of a lagoon, and didn't get back on—she could handle it now. And yet not be part of it. And yet have her own happy, quiet spot.

She just needed more time, that was all. To make it her spot. It had taken her a while to find her spot in the islands, too—she'd made a disastrous mess of her first year, in fact, to the point that she'd had to change islands. She just tended to forget that now, to think only of the way it had been at the end, of that happy, supportive community that had grown over three years around her, like the vines growing up this stone. Or maybe her community there had been the stone, and she'd been the clinging vine.

Luc was all alone, too, she thought, as she stepped into the old stone alley behind the restaurant. Clothes hanging on lines between the balconies above layered stripes of shadow across the sunlight that slipped down into the narrow alley, and the cobblestones were bumpy underfoot. Luc had brought a few of his old staff down with him, young men to whom the thought of leaving Paris for the sunny south appealed. But most of them had stayed up in Paris. And, of course, Patrick hadn't come.

Luc knew almost no one here, other than the men he employed or the suppliers with whom he worked. Slow friendships might be forming, but Luc was Luc, after all: contained and perfectionist, so impossible at opening up. He had mentioned a former chef of his who had a restaurant around here, Gabriel Delange, but hadn't yet even managed to see the other man, both intensely busy chefs in separate restaurants in separate towns.

Did he give himself time to feel lonely? Or did he just work too hard, focus too intensely on his creations?

Maybe all he had was her.

It wasn't a good thing, that she be his one source of happiness outside of work, and yet thinking of it made her soften still further, a golden longing to see him, to hold him, to find a moment when she wasn't throwing up and he wasn't working to just ask him: *Luc, is something wrong? Can I kiss it and make it better?*

He liked those kisses that made things better. Sometimes, when she bandaged some kitchen wound for him at the end of a hard day, he liked it so much that he had to sit down. He would pull her between his legs and wrap the non-wound-bearing arm around her waist and just hold on tight, his head buried in her breasts.

Sometimes she teased him by taking his hand and finding the tiniest nicks and scratches to stroke, until he was almost ill with how much he liked it, this wondering sugar-overdose, this incredulous hunger.

She would like to do that right now. She missed his hands. She wanted his hands to learn someday to take the touch of hers for granted.

The sounds of the kitchens echoed down the alley— clashes of metal and calls of *Service* or *Chaud, chaud, chaud*—as Summer made her way to the back door. The scents roiled around her like worms suddenly, and she clapped a hand to her stomach. *Not again. Behave.*

The nausea was probably why Luc had rejected her the night before, really. It wasn't his fault. Talk about a turn-off, Jesus. He was a sweetheart, and he'd worked extra hard to reassure her about it, but clearly some things were difficult for a man to stomach.

It had reminded her of the old days, when he used to reject her, but *it wasn't like that at all*, as she had repeated to herself over and over while he fell asleep and she lay awake worrying.

Silly worries. How did she manage to make such a big deal out of things in the dark hours of the night?

She stepped into the doorway. Luc. Her whole body lightened when she saw him, his attention focused utterly on something he was making, some pale white sphere with the faintest tint of green, and raspberries.

His graceful, intense movements always seemed to cut the shadows in the room to pieces, until they slunk to the corners in awe and stared at him. The long, lean, elegant, muscled form of him, so graceful and so ruthless with the demands he made on himself. A mortal man so determined to be a god. She'd called him the Lord of Hell once, for that fire-forged purity of his face, the beautiful high cheekbones, the golden skin. But he wasn't the Lord of Hell. He was just a man. Her man. This incredible, extraordinary man who had given himself to her. Who had let her steal everything he had ever accomplished away from him and force him to start over here, where she could be happy.

So she was supposed to be happy. And right now, watching him, she was.

The beauty of his focus had always lured her so powerfully that it had taken practice on her part not to just force herself into the center of that concentration in her desperate need to make herself its heart.

I'm already its heart. Over and over he tried to teach her that, this precious knowledge—that she was the heart of everything he did. *He might even be making that for me.*

The green-white sphere, fresh from a dip in liquid nitrogen, looked like an oasis of crisp, cool freshness, there across the intense, bustling kitchen, the same way Luc was an oasis of dark control. That perfect gorgeous profile would turn in a moment. He would see her. He would smile, and she would make her way to him as if that smile parted hell and led her through it straight to his heart.

Her phone beeped, and she hesitated a long moment, but then pulled it out. Another message from her mother. She needed to turn off the alerts on that thing.

But now that she had seen it, she just kept *craving*...something. Something feminine and supportive, some maternal promise that everything was fine, that she wasn't the first generation to have a baby. Luc was right there. If her mother said one of her more mind-wrecking things, Summer could talk to him. Touch him. Watch him work. That always relaxed everything about her.

She took a breath, and more scents crept into her, wriggling unpleasantly in her stomach. But she read the text.

PS I haven't told your father yet, I promise. We'll wait until it's sure. Or better yet, until you know the sex, so he won't get his hopes up for a boy like he did with you. You know how long he stays disappointed about that kind of thing. (Smiley face.) Love you, sweetie!"

"Chaud!" a man called, passing with a great pan of madeleines straight from the oven, lemon and butter crawling through the air, thick and strong. And *"Chaud!"* another chef called, a whirl of white chef's jacket and the thick, buttery, sweet scent of caramel as he passed with a pot.

The great wormy mass of scents roiled into her mouth, clogging it until she could barely stop herself from gagging. She stared at Luc across those odors, so close, if she could make it ten steps she could touch him. And everything would be all right. *Just breathe.* But at the breath, the wiggling odors stuffed themselves down her throat, and she dove back down the alley, making it half a dozen steps before she bent over a jasmine planter, gagging dryly.

Nothing came up but a thin bit of ghastly bile, her stomach already emptied by the salon, but her body heaved and heaved trying to make something come out, until she finally could sink down to her butt on the cobblestones, pulling her knees up, her back against the wall, pressing her damp face into her hands. Tears pricked her eyes, at the way her own body defeated her. God, this throwing up thing was exhausting. As if the baby was trying to beat her down into something limp and resistless so it could swell in her, take her over.

It kind of reminded her of being harangued by her dad, actually, when he was pissed at her—broken down into nothing, over and over and over.

When the nausea calmed finally, she rolled her head wearily against the wall behind her, enough to gaze up the alley at the restaurant back door. Sounds still carried to her. Yells from one end of the kitchens to another. Clashes of pans. The fast, repeated banging of someone settling macarons onto their sheets. A calm resonance that prickled over her skin—Luc.

She curled her knees up to her chest and sat there a long time, listening for that rare vibration of Luc's voice raised enough for her to hear it this far away. *Talk louder, Luc. I can't hear you. Yell at somebody like most chefs would do.*

But Luc never needed to yell. That firm command of his carried over the whole kitchen when he made it. And almost, almost reached far enough to brush against her skin.

She sighed, closing her eyes. Luc worked so hard. He needed to be able to focus. He wanted to win his baby a star. A little smile twitched her lips as she remembered his face as he'd said it, so vulnerable and hopeful.

He was *such* a sweetheart, under all that control of his. He needed her support. She couldn't be spoiled and needy and complain that she needed more of his time.

She was only pregnant, Jesus. Women did it all the time. According to her mother, it wasn't even that sure of a thing.

She slipped her hand over her belly, to shield it from her mother's words and the whole world. Her whole body tightened—her skin, her hand on her belly, the muscles in her butt against the cobblestones, her back against the wall—in need of someone to talk to.

A visit to her island. The more she thought about it, the more that seemed like such a good idea. She could let Luc concentrate, not bother him with her ridiculous, clingy nerves, and just take a week to relax, to get her head back on straight.

The women there would laugh at her, they would tease her, they would be happy for her. She closed her eyes, as she leaned against the wall, imagining it so vividly her whole body relaxed into it.

Just a little trip. Luc wouldn't even miss her.

Chapter 12

"A critic," Luc said. "From *Nice-Matin*." The big regional papers were the worst. They just had to prove their superiority over Paris chefs.

Damn it, where was Summer? Why hadn't she come in today? He had designed a lime sphere for her that she would *love*. He hoped. Since suddenly now she liked lime.

Nicolas shrugged his stocky shoulders as if he'd just been shearing three hundred unruly sheep. No critic in France, New York, or Tokyo would ever have expected to find Luc Leroi working with a chef who came across as a philosopher-farmer, but Luc figured Nico's handful-of-earth approach didn't have to be incompatible with his jewels-of-creation one. After all, that was where you found jewels, right? In the earth. They'd get the balance between them right soon. He liked what the man was doing too much to want to separate from him already, before they had properly tried.

"That's what my cousin said," Nicolas said cheerfully. "Sounds as if the review is lined up for Sunday's paper, so you know they have to be coming in tonight or tomorrow."

Right. Damn it.

He glanced at the clock. *Merde.* Their house wasn't even that far away. That was the whole point, to have it only a couple of streets over from the restaurant so it would be easy for Summer to stop by, for Luc to get home to her. But minutes could count as hours in the restaurant business. He could accomplish a lot in a minute.

And his team as yet could not even reliably temper chocolate. Apparently. *Damn it*, he needed Patrick.

"You know, one of these days I need to get home to my wife," he said acerbically. "Figure out what to name the baby."

Talk to her. Except what if she tells me something is wrong?

Nico stopped dead. "What to name—*merde*. Really?" He grinned, grabbed Luc, and pulled him into a great hug. "When?"

"Just the other day," Luc said, totally confused. Had somebody just hugged him? It *felt* that way, but—what? He and Nico were practically strangers. Actually, maybe that was why Nico had done such a weird thing. Nobody who knew him hugged him. Even Patrick only pretended hugs, and that was just to throw Luc off-kilter.

Nico's beam grew. "Really? You just learned it? No wonder you're acting so crazy."

Luc was acting crazy? That was, in a way other people could tell? "I think I always act like this."

"You do? *Merde.*" Nico stared at him with a mix of incredulous pity and respect.

Luc frowned.

"But I meant, when's it due?" Nico asked.

"February."

Nico whistled a little. "You gave yourself a really tight deadline for getting this restaurant in shape to run without you, didn't you? *That's* why you're so intense."

Luc stared at him a full ten seconds before he could even come up with a response. "I'm always—did you actually do any research about who I *am* before you agreed to take this job?"

Nico grinned. Sometimes Luc had the impression that Nico found him very amusing. Like a cute baby lamb that was still finding its legs. Given that they were roughly the same age and Luc was the one who'd already landed three stars in his life, it was pretty damn annoying. "Luc Leroi, right. I was a little worried about it. I mean you're photogenic and all that, so you look great on television, but are you any good with *food*?"

Luc's lips parted. He didn't ever actually do that—lose control of any part of his body, right down to whether his lips were pressed together or not—but he'd just been sucked down a rabbit hole. *Was...he...*had Nico spent that ten-year gap in his résumé locked up in an insane asylum? He'd always thought those obscure references to a family farm that Nico had made during the interview seemed vague.

"But it's okay," Nico said reassuringly. Luc could practically feel his baby lamb wool being petted. "You're a little obsessive, but you do all right."

"I—do—all *right*?" Words entirely failed him.

"With the food, I mean." Nico made a fist and bumped Luc's stomach lightly. Maybe Nico was smoking something? That would explain the easy-going manner. Lots of chefs did, after hours, to release the adrenaline, but if he was doing it while he was actually *on*—shit. Luc would have to find a new chef. *Merde,* that was the last thing he needed. "Deep down here, you still respect it. You still remember it's food. And that the whole point of it isn't to make people say what a god you are, but just to feed them and make them happy."

Luc just stood there. There were so many things to think about in what Nico had just said that suddenly all he could think about was Summer: her face that first time she realized that he truly meant these desserts not to control her, not even to make her fall in love with him, but just to make her happy. Maybe it had been the first time she realized it because it was also the first time it was true.

He thought of her face as he slid that chocolate tulip well toward her, that metaphor for trapping her with him where she couldn't get away, and of the revulsion he'd caught on her face as she pushed it from her.

Maybe...maybe she'd been right to push it away.

Damn it, where was she?

"I mean, Paris chef and all," Nico said easily. "You can't blame me for having some reservations. But at heart, you're not so bad."

Luc's brain was going to explode. It didn't have synapses for this.

"Nico. We're trying to be a three-star restaurant here. Obsessiveness, intensity—that's how it *works*. We did talk about the star goal when I—when you came on?" He'd almost said *when I hired you,* oops. Luc knew better than to emphasize who was hiring whom with a chef de cuisine. He was lucky he could find a good one willing to work *for* the pastry chef in the first place.

"Yeah, I thought it would be interesting. And it is," Nico added thoughtfully. He picked up one of the white freestone peaches he'd brought in that morning for Luc, having collected the fresh-fallen fruit on the edge of a field on his way in, and sliced it with absent deftness. He bit into a slice. "Mmm. Perfect. Fresh from the tree like that. You can't even get them that ripe at a little farmer's market. They bruise too easily." He held another slice out to Luc.

Luc looked at that callused hand holding the gleaming white slice out to him, confused. But then he took it and bit into it and...damn, that was good.

Just for a second, all his world slowed down, and he closed his eyes, lost in how good it was.

"But sometimes," Nico said, "I'd rather be doing that."

Luc's eyes opened. Nico was watching him rather quizzically and with considerable satisfaction. As if he wanted to pat the little lamb on the head. "What?"

"That." Nico nodded at him. "What I just did."

Luc stared at him. His mouth watered. He wanted another slice of that damn peach.

Nico smiled and put the whole fruit into his hand, the remaining slices falling gently away from the seed into Luc's palm as he released it.

"A family style restaurant," Nico said, as he headed back to his side of the kitchen. "Where kids can come and laugh and wander among tables. Or maybe a farmhouse kitchen, with hungry hands pouring in at the end of the day. Or a soup kitchen." He shrugged as he disappeared and then leaned back with a quick, reassuring smile for the lamb: "But don't worry. You're pretty interesting so far. Although—I don't mean to be giving advice, since you won't appreciate it, but you might want to think about finding time to talk about baby names with your wife." He disappeared again.

Luc stared after him. Then he looked down at the white peach falling apart in juicy petals in his hand. He took another slice before he could help himself. God, that tasted so damn good. And it made him think of Summer again. How she liked fresh fruit. How the first thing he had ever made her that she'd eaten had been when he *listened* to her, listened to how much she was missing her island, and sliced up a mango.

Damn it, *where was she?*

He stepped out of the back door of the kitchens, restlessly, just to take a moment alone with his peach and breathe, and stopped very still.

His wife was sitting halfway down the cobblestone alley, her back against the ochre wall of a house, jasmine climbing up the wall beside her, shadows and sunlight flickering across her face from the breeze-stirred clothes someone had hung in the narrow gap between balconies above her. She had a laptop on her knees, but it was closed, and she looked as if she was fast asleep.

His heart started to thump very hard. There was something incredibly beautiful about the combination of elements—Summer and the jasmine and the Provençal alley—a picture that should be in a calendar. But even he could tell that something about it was all wrong.

Chapter 13

"Summer." Summer smiled. The warm sunlight and scent of jasmine, and that dark, quiet voice. Luc had found her. He'd come to her island with her. Part of all the smiling, happy people. Now they could *all* celebrate the baby together. "Summer."

His voice soothed her, as it always had. From the very first moment she met him, even when her heart was thumping with the tension of their battles, some part of her had always been drawn to bury herself in his arms, in that sense of utter security that his dark control brought her.

She smiled at him and opened her eyes, and the island skewed around her like a camera gone out of focus, and when its focus righted, she wasn't on an island at all, but in a Provençal alley. Luc wasn't in those cut-offs he'd made out of his Dior jeans when he came to find her on her island, he was squatting beside her in the alley in that stylized shirt he favored, the one made with sturdy cloth like any chef's jacket but with a collar that made him look, on camera, as if he was just home from the theater or something.

He did have that exact same look on his face that he'd had when they'd first come face to face on her island, though: grave, intent, searching, all that feeling packed up tight in him, held in control. But there. So much feeling, so intense, that he didn't know how to handle it all if he started letting it all out.

Still half in her dream, half on that island with him, she gave him a smile shaped like the invitation to a kiss. *Come here, Luc. You can let it all out with me.*

"Summer," he said again, voice very gentle, and she started fully awake, scrambling up into a straighter sitting position against the wall as she realized where she was. Her butt lanced pain through her at the shift in position on the cobblestones, and her face flooded with shame.

I'm sorry I'm so pathetic. I'm sorry I'm so clinging and needy when you're doing so fine without me.

"Peach?" He stretched out a hand to her, the slices flowering in it, juicy and white.

Oh, wow, that looked—that looked *delicious*. Her mouth watered as it hadn't in days, not since those pickles, as if food could actually be *good*. She snatched a slice from him and sank her teeth into it.

That was so good. She closed her eyes to concentrate on it.

When she swallowed, a thumb touched her lower lip gently, and then another slice of peach nudged her lips. She parted them, her eyes still closed, sucking the peach inside her mouth, savoring it. Sweet and sunshine and a promise of happiness.

He still loved her then. Loved *her*, the woman who didn't always do what he wanted, who sometimes just needed fruit and a kiss. Opening her eyes, she made a little kissing motion with her lips, and he leaned forward. When his lips touched hers, the scents on him swirled around her and her stomach swirled with them. Uh-oh.

Oh, crap. If she couldn't even handle the scents on him from the restaurant, that was going to be bad.

He leaned back, and she drew a quick breath of jasmine and stone. Scents she could handle.

"Summer." Black eyes watched her with that utter intensity of his. "What are you doing here?"

"I just started feeling a little sick," she said hastily. *I haven't been sitting here for an hour just so I can almost hear you talk or anything.*

His voice was so perfectly suited to the darkness of her closed lids. "Why didn't you come inside?"

"I tried." There was no good way to tell him this. "The scents got to be a bit much for me." She peeked at him.

Shock ran across his face. "You can't come into the *restaurant?* That's—" Panic flashed in his eyes, and then he ran a hand through his hair and gave his head a shake, tightening control back over his face. "That's just a fluke, right? Just today?"

"I don't know." She gazed at the peach slices still in his hand. Did she dare eat another one? Those two had been so good. But the scents on him had kicked her stomach up again, and so far, that never seemed to end well for her. "It seems to be getting worse."

"*How* long does morning sickness last?"

"On the web, it said a little bit past the first trimester. But in the forums, a lot of women said theirs had lasted much longer than that, sometimes even the whole pregnancy."

"In the forums?"

She took another peach and drew it into her mouth, concentrating on its sweet sunshine rather than the words it stopped her from saying: *I don't have anyone else to ask, Luc.*

Yes, I'm terrible at making friends. You're the only person on this continent who likes me. You *have a place, but my only place is through you.*

And I'm losing even that. Because I can't control my damned body.

Because I want to cling.

Maybe she was just weak. Maybe a stronger woman would master morning sickness. If she knew any strong women here, she could ask them.

"The guys really miss you when you don't come." Luc's darkest, quietest voice. The one she always felt she could curl up safe in. The one that always made her feel as if *she*, everything about her, was entirely okay. Loved by him.

She looked up, blinking, almost in tears.

"My staff." He gestured back to the back door of the restaurant. "Especially the apprentices. They love showing off for you when you come in. You know they love you."

Her face softened. They did seem to, yes. But if she walked into that restaurant, she would have to eat whatever they offered her to make them happy, just as she had to do with Luc. Her stomach roiled just at the thought.

"They've never met anyone as patient and gentle and giving in their whole lives." Dark eyes watched her intently. "That's not common, Summer, to take a brain as bright as yours and be willing to sit down and patiently coach people how to read, while you smile, and praise, and make them feel as if *they're* the ones doing something special for you."

"They are," Summer said, surprised. How to explain? "They make me feel—whole." *Right. A good, happy person. A person who could be a good mother, who could just be a good part of this world.* "I'll meet them at the playground by the *pétanque* courts." A flat area at the top of the town, where old men played *boules* and the wind swept the air clean of all scents but pine and stone and a hint of sea. "We can work on their lessons there."

He nodded and looked down a moment. The slant of sun that made its way into the alley gleamed off his black hair, filling it paradoxically with light. "I miss you, too," he told the cobblestones. He caught himself immediately. "But don't worry about that. I can manage for a few weeks. I'm not a—baby." His eyes flicked to her stomach and then lingered there. He stretched out a hand to caress her flat belly just lightly.

Summer rested her head against the wall and watched him, while all his focus was on her belly.

Aww. Hey. Just for a second there, his controlled face was so wondering and exposed. His long, thick lashes were so black against his gold cheeks, his hand so warm against her belly. *Cup more firmly, Luc. Take possession. Say, This baby is mine.* "Are you happy about the baby, Luc?" she asked softly.

His gaze flicked back to hers, as if she had caught him in some kind of criminal act. "Of course," he said quickly.

Too quickly.

She drew a breath, pulling her knees up higher until his hand was locked between her thighs and her belly. *Now* the pressure of his hand was firm, but only because she had trapped it. *He's lying!*

Oh, God.

She didn't even have *him* with her for this pregnancy. She was making a baby, and she was *all alone.*

All alone. Her worst nightmare.

That loneliness she had risked for him. Because his love was supposed to be enough to keep her safe from it.

"Have you eaten anything else today?" he asked.

She shrugged uncomfortably, still focused on that lie. *He's not happy? He's not happy.*

"You can't spend the next six weeks or more eating only peaches!" he snapped, his face hardening.

Peaches sounded like a lot more nourishment than she'd managed so far today. God, she hated it when people tried to tell her what she could or couldn't eat. Her whole being revolted.

Fuck you for not being happy, Luc. You begged *me for this. And now it's happening in* my *body.*

"If I can even keep this down," she managed.

That slashing, beautiful frown. He used to frown a lot at her. Look her over with cool dismissive eyes as if she was nothing. "Summer, how can you not keep a peach down? It's light and fresh and—"

She rolled over onto her knees suddenly, gagging. It wrenched her body, and she *hated* it. God, she hated it. She hated most that it had to happen in front of Luc, and she sagged afterward, with her forehead pressed against the stone, not looking at him. "Like that, I guess," she muttered, trying again not to cry.

A heavy, warm hand stroked her back. "Summer. This is insane."

"I asked the doctor." Scheduled an appointment, sat there in the waiting room, explained her problem while the doctor looked at her as if she was an idiot. *You're pregnant. That's what pregnancy is like. You'll be lucky if it doesn't last six months, like it did me.* "She said it was normal."

His eyes crinkled. "You went to see the doctor again?"

Well, yes. At least it was someone to talk to.

"You didn't even tell me you'd gone." Luc stared at her.

She shrugged. *When would I? Either you're working or I'm throwing up. Yeah, it's not exactly the cozy picture of family life I imagined.*

Well…to be truthful, it was the one she had imagined in her dark moments, when all she could see was herself repeating the cycle her parents had started in her. But it wasn't the one she imagined when she believed in herself and Luc and had hope.

Luc watched her for a moment, frowning. "Did she say anything that would *help*?"

Summer shrugged again. His hand rode her shoulder muscles with the movement, and her loneliness eased. "She said different women had different little tricks, but there wasn't any magic cure. She can give me medicine if it gets really impossible, but I'm not sure I know what impossible is. I *think* most women just get through this." Longing rose in her again for female voices swapping stories, so that she would *know*. Know what it was like, know how they did it, know when she was supposed to see a doctor or just tough it up.

Luc made a face. "Could medicine hurt the baby?"

"I don't know. That's why I'm not taking it."

Heavy petting, up and down her back, easing the nausea more than any other thing could. "Do you think you would like to come sit on the restaurant terrace? We

81

could take you through the front where the smells aren't so strong. Or do you want me to walk you home?"

She did want to sit on the restaurant terrace. Even if it wouldn't be anywhere near him really, while he worked, it *seemed* more a part of things. So much better than being in their home by herself, looking at internet forums on pregnancy and trying to get through the day's nausea. But getting to that terrace seemed so hard. She rolled back over into a sitting position, slumping. "I kind of like it right here," she whispered.

"Summer." Luc's face twisted in frustrated distress.

"I just wish you'd talk more loudly," she muttered. "When you're working in there."

"What?"

"Nothing."

He stared at her a moment, black eyes trying to see into her soul. She offered him a weak smile, not her best effort, but the bouts of nausea didn't leave her with much inside her, not even smiles. "Don't worry about it," she said. "I'm not the first woman to survive pregnancy, you know. I'll manage."

"Right." He crouched, frowning at her. "Right."

"I will, Luc. I'll manage on my own." *You're the only person this baby can count on, Summer. You've got to be strong.*

And her baby needed a swing.

***

Or he would manage for her, Luc thought, as he went back to the kitchens. Just to be on the safe side. At least he knew he could always count on himself.

Limes, he noted on a sheet of paper pinned to the corkboard near his work station. *Peaches. Raspberries. Mangoes??* On the computer in his office, which was set to favor American sites because Summer was its primary user these days, he searched tips for controlling nausea. Crackers, all right. Ice pops, well, he was doing that. The mother-to-be could try forcing herself to swallow small bites of protein at regular intervals all morning, for which they recommended...peanut butter?

Surely not. He was trying to avoid foods that made someone feel sick. That was what he got for checking an American site.

Although...Summer *was* American. And she'd wanted those American pickles.

Peanut butter, though. He took a deep breath and stared at the ceiling before he closed his eyes very tightly and then called Sylvain.

"I need Cade."

A pause on the other end of the phone. Then that amused, chocolate voice: "Well, that's unfortunate for you, because you can't have her."

"I just need her to get me some peanut butter from that American store of hers. In case there's some kind they like from their childhood. Probably some Corey subsidiary produces some, right?"

"Luc." Sylvain sounded horrified. "You can't do that to your wife. She probably left that benighted country just so she could *escape* peanut butter. I mean, why else would she have come?" Teasing glowed rich and dark under his words, as if even Sylvain's humor had this base of melted, gleaming chocolate.

"For me," Luc said tensely.

Sylvain sighed. "You know, Luc, sometimes your sense of humor—"

Yes, he had caught the fact that Sylvain was joking, he just didn't find it that funny. It would have been far less responsibility on his shoulders, when he found his wife sitting alone and sick in a damn alley behind his restaurant, if Summer had come to France for any other reason besides or even in addition to him. It would have given him something to fall back on if he failed. *Look, I know things seem bad right now, but at least you've escaped peanut butter!*

Yeah, that was going to work, all right.

A flashing vision of his old sous-chef Patrick getting hold of that peanut butter hope and wickedly twitting Luc with it until Luc had to laugh, until it became genuinely funny, reducing all his gut-deep panic into something silly and manageable. But Patrick was taking courses in math and physics to prepare for engineering while he simultaneously helped cover the transition at the Leucé, a schedule even more insane than Luc's, so it wasn't as if Luc could call on him. And after that he would be going to California. So Luc *really* couldn't call on him. Couldn't let himself need a friend at all. *The best things in my life always leave me.*

A deep breath. "This website I found says sometimes it helps with morning sickness. It's something about the protein."

A moment's blank silence. "Well, couldn't you give her something better? Grind up some hazelnuts, or some almonds, make a nice little *praliné* base—do you need me to come down there and show you how to do this stuff?" Again the humor.

But Luc stopped, standing still on the restaurant terrace looking out to sea. Because—no, obviously. And yet, for some reason, he didn't want to say that no. And he had no idea why he should want Sylvain coming down to interfere in his kitchens with that arrogance of his, acting as if he'd invented chocolate personally and was the only person in the world who could properly handle anything to do with it.

"I'm going to try some other things, too. The peanut butter is extra. In case she only likes a certain brand from her childhood or—look, can you just ask Cade?"

"Sure," Sylvain said, amused. "You know, all joking aside, you could actually call her directly. I'm a tiny bit more secure than certain people to whom I might be speaking."

Luc looked at his phone rather blankly. Calling another chef's wife directly had never occurred to him as a possible means of communication before. How would he feel if Sylvain called Summer?

Fairly indifferent, he realized on a blink of surprise. For all her past filled with boyfriends, he couldn't even imagine Summer leaving him for another man.

That wouldn't be why she left him.

Tension recoiled, tight and deep. *Why* had his own mother left him? Life just too tough, and she'd preferred to ditch him and his father for the warmth and happiness she found back in her island home? She'd certainly found maternity too much to handle.

Insane Me, please, please, please leave me alone.

I need to be sane for this. I've got to be. I'm going to be a father.

And I'm still trying to figure out how to be a husband.

"So when are you coming to visit?" he asked Sylvain abruptly. "June in Provence. It's a nice time to be down here."

A tiny silence on the other end. They'd been on teams for contests representing France, they'd met in professional associations and worked on charity benefits together. But chefs rarely had time to hang out with other chefs over drinks, and they hadn't ever even had dinner at one another's homes until Cade had dragged Luc and Summer over there in her initial matchmaking attempts. So from there to acting as if a visit to Provence to see them was normal and expected was a bit of a leap.

"Lonely?" Sylvain asked, voice still chocolate-easy but sympathetic. "It's a switch from Paris, isn't it?"

Luc rubbed the back of his neck. "It's for Summer. I think she needs, you know, female friends, right now."

Another little silence, impossible to interpret. "Well, let's see—lavender in bloom, the Mediterranean right there at your doorstep, and a pregnant cousin. I'm pretty sure Cade would be happy for us to take a trip. You're not inviting Dom and Jaime, too, I hope?"

For some reason, out of the blue, Luc started to smile, and that one gesture made all the tension in him ease. "You know you love him."

"I do *not, merde.*" A thumping noise on the other end of the connection, possibly Sylvain's head against something.

Luc's smile grew until it almost felt—relaxed. Enjoying himself. "It will be fun."

Sylvain's groan as he hung up was so expressive that Luc was actually grinning as he left his office. Things were starting to heat up a little as they got closer to lunch hour, Nico's side swinging into full battle mode first, Luc's in a half hour delay after. He poked his head in on Nico. "Good peach," he murmured.

In under half an hour, standing at this spot between the main and pastry kitchens would be like standing between two battle zones, the insane clash of pans and flash of knives and flame on Nico's side, and the more delicate, more intense, equally brutal work on Luc's side, with its own clashes of pans and plenty of flaming torches, smoking liquid nitrogen, boiling caramel and oil. Right now, things were practically calm in comparison. Of course, it was *all* calm in comparison to a luxury hotel kitchen with a hundred cooks on staff. Over all, Luc liked this smaller kingdom, but sometimes his leftover adrenaline didn't know what to do with itself.

Nico, his knife blurring through potatoes as fast as a hummingbird's wing, gave him a quick, pleased smile, without even coming close to cutting his own fingers off or slowing his rhythm. "Yeah?"

"Summer liked it."

"Aww." Nico beamed. "Did I help feed the little baby? Damn. Makes a man feel good about himself, doesn't it?"

It would, yes. If Luc ever managed it. "I don't suppose you have any peanuts over here?"

Nico looked at him blankly. "I thought you said West African dishes didn't go with our style."

86

Maybe Sylvain was right, and he should make a hazelnut butter instead. Surely hazelnuts would be a *much* better flavor, even to a pregnant woman.

"We can order some," Nico said. "Especially if you'll quit being so damn unadventurous about the West African stuff. But it will probably take a few days. They're not exactly common."

Or an almond butter. That would definitely be better than peanut butter. "Those peaches...where did you get them?"

Wait, unadventurous? *Him?* There was a huge difference between being too elegant for peanuts and being unadventurous. He gave Nico one of his cooler looks, the kind that made pretty nearly everybody feel for their necks in this weird gesture, as if a mere look had cut off their heads.

Nico bit back a grin. "You going to go gleaning with me, Luc?"

Oh, God, that sounded like one of those cheap horror films where your past kept sticking its damn hand out of the grave. But...Summer had really loved that peach. It and pickles were the only things he had gotten right in this pregnancy so far. Not that he had been responsible for either one of them—the pickles had been Cade's accomplishment, and the peaches Nico's.

It would be nice if something his wife needed actually came from *him.*

"Sure." He thought the word came out fine. He thought it didn't get stuck in his throat.

Surprise on Nico's face, and then a quick, bemused flick of that hazel gaze over him. "You, uh, going to do it in one of your Dior dress shirts or can I persuade you to put on a T-shirt?"

Luc closed his eyes. "I'll put on a T-shirt." He did actually have some. He wore them under his chef's gear and sometimes on Sundays, when he could relax with Summer. *Sunday.* Pure longing ran through him. *Coming up soon.*

Nico grinned. "Got any jeans with holes in them?"

"Oh, for God's sake." Luc went back to his side of the kitchen.

Chapter 14

Summer waved the apprentices off with a smile and took some deep breaths of the pine and sun and sea breeze. She wouldn't go so far as to say her stomach felt delightful, but it was calmer here, in this open air. The tutoring session maybe hadn't been her best—every time she bent too close to the young men and the cooking scents on them hit her, nausea had stirred again—but the apprentices had seemed to appreciate it anyway.

She closed her books, sneaking a glance at the table of women next to hers. They were laughing and chattering, exclaiming over the belly of the woman with the curly brown hair, who was beaming smugly. It made Summer's chest hurt.

She recognized them vaguely. They crossed paths around town. The child that woman carried would presumably go to school with her own child. They certainly knew *her,* in fact probably thought they knew everything there was to know about Summer Corey and none of it good. And she didn't usually allow other women power over her. She knew how *that* worked out, when she showed other girls she was lonely and desperate for their friendship. Her competitive, rich girl's boarding school had taught her that. No, a silky smile as she strolled past, as if they couldn't even dream of touching her much less hurting her, was by far the best way to handle other women.

But...would all those women's kids grow up to be friends and go to each other's birthday parties, while Summer's was the one everyone hated? Just as people had hated her?

Even though all that lay between their tables was dry, light, pine-scented wind, the barrier felt like this thick, stretchy, transparent thing through which female laughter and solidarity could be seen blurrily but never reached. This elastic and unyielding barrier at which she could push and push but never push her way through.

She took a breath. And then, in the same way she'd learned to push herself out into public over and over at her parents' insistence, with a silky, insouciant smile that hid her intense shyness, she stood and pretended to need to pass their table to leave. She paused, with a careless, friendly smile. "Congratulations," she said to the woman with curly hair, nodding at her hands on her belly.

All four women looked at her with instant, visible chill, and Summer's throat clogged, but she kept her smile. Only the pregnant woman gave a tentative half-smile back, wary but a little curious. "Thank you."

"When is it due?" Summer asked. *Do you know more about this than I do? How nauseated have you been? Did you figure out any tricks to calm your stomach?*

"Just before Christmas," the other woman said.

So six or seven weeks ahead of Summer. Should she tell them? A group of strange women already looking at her with closed expressions? *No.* Their reaction to her approach to their table had told her the answer already. But their solidarity made her so *hungry.* That hunger gnawed in her belly, this terrible ache, until she was afraid if she couldn't feed it, it would hurt her baby, too. That her baby would grow up isolated from all the damn world the same way Summer had. "I'm, ah—" Summer hesitated, and then even good manners couldn't quite cover her shyness as she touched her own belly. "Me, too."

But nobody laughed for Summer. Nobody exclaimed in delight. "Are you?" one of the other women said coolly, as if Summer had just tried to steal something from them.

"*Félicitations,*" the pregnant woman said. A couple of murmurs of *félicitations* followed hers. Then the other women just watched Summer, clearly waiting for her to move on and quit ruining their moment by trying to insert herself into it.

Summer didn't stop smiling, but a knot lodged deep and hard in her throat that she couldn't swallow down. She smiled over it. "I'm, ah, Summer," she tried.

The women exchanged ironic glances. "Yes, we know," one of them said.

Oh.

No one offered a return introduction. Well, why should they? *They* didn't need friends. Definitely not filthy rich, spoiled brat friends with an international reputation that even four years in the South Pacific hadn't lived down.

"When's yours due?" the pregnant woman finally asked politely.

"Early February." A February baby, for two people who had originally agreed to marry each other on Valentine's Day.

"Should you even be telling people yet?" one of the expectant mother's friends asked coolly. "You know what they say."

Summer took a step back, her hand covering her belly. "N-o." *And I don't want to know. I don't want to know what they say.*

The mom-to-be sent her friend an appalled look and pinched her arm. Yeah, because the friend was a bitch. Summer had gotten that part. "*Félicitations,*" Summer said again, her own voice gone cool, too, because *fuck you.* She walked on past the table and across the *place,* determined just to get through an archway and be out of sight, not to cry, damn them. She wouldn't give them that.

And her stupid, stupid hormones were *not* helping with the effort not to cry.

A murmur from table behind her, and a woman's voice exclaiming: "Well, what? The nerve of her, trying to steal all the attention for herself! She doesn't have enough already? She probably isn't even pregnant!"

I hate women. I hate them. I hate them. Summer walked faster. *I want my island.* That island, where she didn't hate other women at all, because they didn't hate her. That island, where she could have hugs that felt soft but strong, that wrapped a feminine scent around her, that said, *We're happy for you, happy to welcome your baby into our world. And don't worry so much. You'll be okay. We did it, and we are. Now here's some monoï oil. Rub your belly every day so you won't have stretch marks, and remember to rub it into the baby's scalp when he's born so he'll have beautiful hair...*

Women's voices, from other conversations she had heard when other women got pregnant, that she tried to pull now from her memory and wrap around herself as if they were for her.

"*Pardon,*" a woman's voice said just behind her, and she stiffened, not wanting to look around in case her eyes were shimmering. The other pregnant woman came even with her and took a deep breath, blinking.

"Sorry," the woman said again. "Sometimes when I move too fast these days I get dizzy. The doctors said it's something about the blood vessels dilating. Have you started feeling sick?"

Summer's gratitude for that tiny connection surged so strongly that it took all her will to strangle it back and not let it come out as a flood of tears. "Yes."

The other woman made a face. "I'm starting to get over that, I think. I could almost look at chocolate the other day. *Croisons les doigts.*" She held up her crossed fingers, smiling awkwardly.

"Well." Summer nodded. "I hope so. Congratulations again." *Thank you. For pretending I'm a human being, too.*

"What Chloë said," the other woman added in a rush. "About not telling people yet. That was just stupid. Don't pay any attention to that."

Summer rubbed her belly involuntarily. "I think I've learned my lesson," she said, low and dry. *But I bet I could tell people on my island.*

She could almost taste it, the sense of happiness that would wrap around her, the exclamations of delight, the encouragement and support. Mamie Louise would be bringing her some magic food that pregnant women could actually eat, like green mangoes with chili powder, and...

Green mangoes with chili powder. She had never even liked them, and all the sudden her teeth ached from the need for the crunch and the pea-apple flavor covered with heat.

You idealize your island too much, Summer. You had to work hard to develop friendships there, too.

Maybe the problem, still, is that you believe in the possibilities for happiness on that island more than you believe in the possibilities here.

"What did *you* eat?" she asked the other woman suddenly.

She made a face. "Not much. Chips. Sorbets some. We've been eating in restaurants a lot, or we go to them, but I usually find out that whatever I was so convinced I wanted at that restaurant is something I can't even stand by the time we actually sit down at the table. But it's been easier than trying to survive the smells from cooking in the house, I guess. I'm starting to get better."

This time Summer's smile was almost spontaneous. "Well, that's good," she said. Her gaze skimmed the other woman's belly again, quickly, curiously, as she tried to imagine that roundness on herself. As she tried to imagine feeling a little better.

"I'm still *very* tired and draggy, though," the other woman said ruefully.

Oh. Was that normal? Not just Summer being...spoiled or something?

Summer wished desperately that she could figure out some way to extend this moment, to develop it into an actual friendship, but she couldn't come up with one single thing. Even her island friendships had taken *time.*

"I'm Summer," she said again suddenly, extending her hand.

"Amélie," said the other woman, and Summer smiled again. She would smile her heart out, if that would help make future friends for her baby.

"And if you want to try our restaurant sometime, when you think you can eat, it's on me," Summer said swiftly.

Amélie looked both pleased and a little confused by this generosity from a near-stranger.

Summer shrugged a little, trying to slide some silk over the moment. "A little present for the baby. To say, 'Welcome'."

"Thank you." The other woman's face softened into a smile.

The two of them stood there a moment, awkwardly.

"Well. Congratulations," the other woman said, having done her part to make up for her friends' behavior.

"You, too," Summer said wistfully and headed back down the cobblestone streets toward their house, leaving the other woman to rejoin her friends and all that excited support.

Still, it gave her a little hope. *Maybe Luc will come home early tonight. And we'll get a chance to talk. To be excited together.*

He does want this baby. He really does.

On a sudden wave of tenderness, she realized that Luc, too, must be bogged down in his own emotions. They packed in him so tightly, and he had so little idea how to handle them beyond making desserts and, these days, making love to her. And, boy, had he ever had a messed-up childhood.

But he'd *loved* the idea of having a baby. His face would just light every time he talked about it, back there when they were on her island, lying in hammocks, planning their future for which he and she would both

94

sacrifice every other happiness and sense of worth they had ever found for themselves. Her island and her teaching. His restaurant in Paris.

That's okay, they'd always said. *We'll have each other.*

***

Asleep, Summer curved toward his side of the bed, one arm around his pillow, her face buried in it. It was one a.m. Again. The damn restaurant was eating him alive.

Luc stood for a moment looking down at Summer. They had had a hard road to reach an understanding of each other, after they first met. But if he had just been able to watch her sleeping back then, just had the courage to relax his heart to what he saw, he would have understood everything about her: beauty and vulnerability, gentleness, and that sweet hunger for him. A willingness to give everything, if only she could have love in return.

He had hardly been able to stand his day, without her at the restaurant in the afternoon. When the apprentices had chattered their way happily out of the restaurant to go meet her at the green café tables by the *boules* court, he'd stared after them with such jealousy. Ready to turn himself back into a lowly apprentice again just for the chance to sit near Summer.

He didn't know how he was going to get through this morning sickness phase, and his anxiety made him feel pathetic. *Merde, tough it up.* She's *the one going through it.*

You're just a particularly ineffective spectator.

He sat on the edge of the bed and, as he reached for her hand, noticed the slim silver remote tucked between her palm and the pillow. He turned to look at their TV.

His stomach clenched. Photos of Summer's island life scrolled there. A close-up of a beautiful gardenia. A photo of Summer sitting at some old giant of a woman's feet, the woman weaving a lei, Summer hugging her knees to her chest, head tilted back to smile up at the older woman. Summer with a pile of black-haired kids spilling all over her, the kids making all kinds of silliness out of their expressions and poses, Summer laughing. His stomach tightened and tightened until he felt like the kid in the Métro again, two days without food, his dad's face blank behind his accordion, and no mother in sight, only all those glossy, polished commuter women who ignored his dancing, ignored his outstretched hand begging for change.

Had his mother had more kids, after she ran back to her island? Had she, too, ended up laughing and happy there, after she had left Luc behind?

He looked down at the present he had carried home with him through the streets: a frozen lime-flavored sphere graced with raspberries. He'd thought about doing a peach sorbet, but he'd wanted it all to come from him, not part from Nico. And, and...*since when do you like lime so much? Since it smells like you.*

He had put his heart into it for her, the way he always did. He liked it when she ate his heart. When she licked the spoon clean of him as if she wanted every last drop of what he was.

The sphere was melting now, no longer perfect. Soon it would be an unsalvageable mess.

Going into the kitchen, he tossed it into the sink and stood there staring at it, as it slowly melted away. As the last lump of sorbet slid slowly down the drain, he bent over the sink and clutched his head in his hands, trying to breathe himself sane.

In the bedroom, he stopped suddenly. The island photos were still scrolling randomly. And there was their wedding, both of them garlanded with tiare flowers. They held each other's hands, the priest just beyond them with his hand upraised. Summer's face was radiant, tilted up to his own. She looked so happy—relieved, delighted, amazed, as if she couldn't believe something this wonderful had happened to her. Something as wonderful as *marrying him*. His own face was wondering, luminous, as if love shone as an actual light from her face and spilled over him.

Slowly, he began to strip down to his briefs, watching those photos. There they were at the pig roast afterward, seated on the ground, Summer leaning into him in some moment of laughter, his arm around her shoulders, pulling her closer. There they were dancing, and around them, also draped in leis, Patrick and Sarah, Dom and Jaime, Sylvain and Cade, even Summer's "Uncle" Mack, who'd flown out there for it when her own parents "hadn't been able to make it". In the photo, Mack Corey, who made a flower lei look like the ultimate in self-confident, powerful male attire, was just in the process of cutting in on Luc. Summer was laughing with pleasure at the attention and Luc was smiling, relaxed, stepping back to allow his honorary uncle-in-law to partner his wife, not afraid he would lose her because he had to let her go for a moment.

Ease seeped through him. Why...he was part of her island happiness. It was, in fact, his happiness, too. How was he forgetting that? He couldn't lose her to something she loved to share with him.

He slipped into bed beside her, propping on his elbow to watch her. Moonlight gilded over her hair and the one visible cheekbone. Gently, he stroked over her cheekbone, down to her lips. So soft. They curved upward in her sleep under the touch of his thumb. Was it bad of him to keep stroking, to hope to wake her up without admitting it? His hands were so callused, compared to hers. He could make his touch as delicate as a butterfly's wing but its texture would always have that roughness. *I love you so damn much. I'd do anything for you. Tell me what to do.*

A sigh ran through her body, her smile deepening. "Luc," she said and kissed the heel of his palm, opening her eyes.

Everything in him relaxed in a rush of utter bliss. His world righted itself. "*Soleil.*" He rubbed her lips, tugging the lower one a tiny bit. "How are you feeling?"

"Yucky." She smiled wryly and kissed his fingertips. Funny how sweet that little gesture still felt, even after months of getting used to it. Months. They had met less than half a year ago, and they were having a baby, and— God, that was such a frantically pretentious claim on a lifetime of happiness. Happiness had given him a passing nod and he'd rushed out and told the world they were lifetime best friends. "Thank you for the raspberries you sent over earlier."

"You liked them?" Maybe he shouldn't have thrown that lime sphere and its raspberries out. That lime sphere that said *I'll take care of you. I'll take the best care I possibly can. You'll be happy with me. Just stay.*

"They helped," she said, which wasn't quite as enthusiastic an answer as he had hoped for, but that could be good enough for him.

He looked at her mouth, imagining it closing around a raspberry, imagining the tart, sweet flavor on her tongue. He bent his head and kissed her, trying to taste it, hours too late.

Her lips parted, and he took over, tasting her, hungry, growing hungrier, until finally it penetrated that she was pushing on his shoulders, trying to twist her mouth free.

He jerked back, the blow deep into his vital parts. "What?" Oh, shit, was he making her want to throw up again?

She pulled a great lock of her hair across her nose, breathing through it, her eyes wincing over it. God, that was—was that *revulsion* when she looked at him? "Luc. I'm sorry, I—it's just the scents. From the restaurant. I can't—"

It took him still another second to realize that she meant *him*. He...stank to her.

When that was what his world *was*, that she loved the way he smelled, she loved the way he felt, she loved his touch, his taste, she loved him. "I thought—yesterday you said—about the lime smell—"

"I'm sorry," she said desperately. Her eyes said it, too: *Please, I'm sorry, I'm so sorry. Don't be mad. I can't help it.*

He took a deep breath, sliding back out of the bed. "No. It's all right. Stop, Summer. It's all right." He reached out to touch her cheek again and caught himself in case his hand stank, too. "I'll go take a shower."

Standing under the water felt so strange. He took a shower every night, of course, after the heat of the kitchens. He often thought of her while he rinsed himself off, of how her hands were going to feel against his fresh, naked skin. Sometimes he shaved at that hour just so his jaw would be smooth as a baby's against her body. And sometimes he didn't, so it would be prickly and he could oh-so-gently scrape it up the inside of her forearm as he held it above her head.

But showering now, at her request, because if he didn't it would make her sick, felt as if he was washing everything of himself away: all the things he had made that day, all the things he had been, the impossible top chef who demanded miracles from everything he touched, who demanded miracles from himself and got them. All of that gone, the scent of lime, the crush of raspberries, the nuts, the caramel, the sugar, the butter, the lavender and rose, the chocolate, the thyme, his sweat, his effort, everything gone. And yet when it was all washed away, he was still there.

He actually hadn't even *shrunk*. He was exactly the same size.

Naked. He ran his hand over his chest, that strange strength and solidity of his body that persisted even when all his accomplishments were washed off it. Then he grasped the showerhead, forcing himself to hold still while it washed him clean, hanging from it as the water ran over him, trying to focus on water and relaxing muscles and nothing else.

A hand stroked gently down his back, through the water, and he started. The hand stroked all the way down his spine as he arched for it, and then curved around one buttock, which clenched. "God, that's hot," Summer murmured.

He licked water off his lips, fallen on them when his head arched back, and didn't let himself turn around, didn't let himself lower his hands from their grip on the showerhead above him. If something about this pose was hot, he didn't want to ruin it.

A shift of air currents. A warm, slight body pressed up against his wet back, and his breath hissed in. His whole body tightened, groin, butt, hands on the showerhead, everything.

"Really hot," Summer said against his back, the words a movement of her lips against his skin. She licked a drop of water off him, and he tightened his grip on the showerhead, burying his face in one arm.

"I love your back." She nuzzled and licked the words across it, just below his shoulder blades, making his muscles flinch with delight. "It's so strong and so smooth." Her hands slid around his body as she spoke, her breasts pressing against his middle back. Her palms stroked—upward. *Damn,* complained his dick. Sometimes his dick was so greedy it got the hell on his nerves. The rest of his body wanted its share, too.

But you could slide one hand down, his dick begged plaintively, straining. *Just one. One for me.* It was all he could do not to grab one of her hands and put it where he wanted it. But he liked so much, at the same time, drawing out the tantalizing physical curiosity about what path her hands would take on their own.

Her fingers knit their way through his chest hair, massaging into him, and he licked his lips as she reached his nipples. Oh-so-lightly, her fingers glanced over his nipples, passed on, came back, and circled round. She knew exactly how to drive him crazy.

"Summer, don't—" He forced a breath in as her hands froze at the word *don't.* "Don't fake it." *Shut the hell up,* his dick said. *What do we care if she fakes it?* But Luc had always cared. His penis had always argued with him, and his mind had always imposed that whiplash order on its straining animal hunger: *She will not fake it with* me. "If you don't want to, if you don't feel all right, I—"

All her kissing and stroking had stilled. "Fake it?" she said stiffly.

Oh, fuck, he had ruined it. His body ran riot, a flood of hormones that tried to kill his brain once and for all. *Just leave us the fuck alone and let us enjoy this,* his hormones beat the revolt at his dictatorial brain. "Never mind."

She bit his back, very gently, just this tiny challenge of teeth. "What do you think I'm faking, Luc?" Her hand slid downward in a curious, twisting path over his chest.

Hell. He took deep breaths, trying to focus. He had a relentless focus. Right now, it was honing in on nothing but her hand, sliding against wet skin, only a few centimeters above his dick. "Nothing," he whispered. Oh, God, he hoped.

One finger—just one—finished that trail down to his penis and slid lightly, tantalizingly to its tip. "And why would I fake?" she asked.

Yeah, he'd pissed her off with that one.

"I don't know," he said roughly. "To—please me."

"Oh, to *please* you." She brought her thumb into play, this maddeningly gentle, squeezing exploration of the blunt tip of his penis. "Well, we wouldn't want *that,* would we? I mean, God forbid I should please you."

"Summer, please..."

"No, no, no." She gave his damn dick a little scolding finger tap and lifted her hand away. "We wouldn't want to start pleasing."

Shit. He pressed his face into his arm, gripping that showerhead for all he was worth. "I take it back. Do whatever you want."

Wait. How had his hormones just *won*?

Her hand hovered, as if uncertain of its right to touch. "*Whatever* I want? Are you sure?"

"I just—oh, God, Summer don't stop."

"No?" A thread of fresh intrigue in her voice.

It licked at him, that intrigue. Licked right over his dick, which leapt for it. He wanted to turn around and grab her, and even more than that, he wanted to find out what she was going to do to him if he held still. "I don't even care," he said helplessly, pressing his forehead into the bend of his elbow as he gripped the showerhead, his muscles straining. "I don't even care if you're doing it to please me."

"You don't?" she murmured, her hand circled around him fully. "How interesting, Luc." There was a hint of a wicked smile in her voice as teeth caught at the skin of his back and nipped again.

Oh, yeah. Do that again. His hips surged against her hand. "Please me," he said roughly into his elbow. "*Merde.* Yes. I want you to."

"Do you," she murmured, drawn out, lingering, just the way her hand lingered in its stroking path up him and back down. "And you don't even care if I'm pretending?" Her hand slipped down and cupped under his penis, a full but gentle hold of his balls. He jerked in pleasure.

"I care," he ground out, into his arm. But—

"Are you sure? What if I tell you I'm faking it right now, Luc? And that I don't want to do this?" Her hand rubbed, gentle and lazy.

He frowned fiercely into the bend of his arm. He did care. He would *not* let her fake it with him. He wouldn't, he wouldn't, he—

"Would you want me to stop?" She withdrew her hand.

"No." The word expelled harshly against his arm. "Summer. Please."

"Ah." She licked his back again, like a reward. And her hand came back to his erection, curling around it, her thumb riding the length of it in one kind, cruel stroke. "So you would want me to keep doing this, even if I'm hating every second of it?"

"Summer." Her hand fisted him and drew slowly the length and back. "Damn you."

Her other hand slid back around to his back, and then down, to clutch hard into one buttock as she drew her fist back up his erection. "Would you or wouldn't you, Luc?"

"*Yes.* Yes, damn it." The water beat down onto his head and back, too hot. Was it beating on her head, running in rivulets around her face pressed against him? "Oh, God, I think part of me would *like* it. Like you doing this to me as some kind of game."

"Well, there's where we run into a problem, Luc." She squeezed his butt hard, then ran her hand under and between his legs to cup his testicles as she stroked up and down his penis again. "Because I'm not really hating any second of it. But it's true that now it's become a little bit of a game."

"I'm going to make you come so hard after this, Summer," he swore into the corded muscles of his arm. "I don't care if you like it right now or not. You *will* before I'm done with you."

"Oh, now, *that's* my Luc," she murmured, playing with pure malice with just the tip of his penis and nothing more, rubbing and rubbing over the tip.

So much helpless pleasure surged through him, all mixed up between arousal and that way she had said "my Luc". *Yes, I'm yours. That much hasn't changed at least?*

And you're mine. I'll show you in just a minute, Summer. I'll make you beg.

"You know what I want you to imagine, Luc?" She turned her palm from him long enough to let water fill it, then wrapped all that wetness back around his penis and let the water spill from her fingers as she drew them tight up the length of him and back. "That all this hot, tight wetness"—she went up on tiptoe and grazed her teeth across his nape—"is my mouth," she whispered, hot, just behind his ear.

"Don't you *dare*." He would come too fast, he would like it too much. He'd never let her do that to him. He couldn't treat Summer that way. *Oh, shit, yeah, he could. If she dropped to her knees right now...*

A laugh against his back. That drove him *crazy*. She was still enough in control to *laugh*? To be *having fun*? "I can't even suck on a Popsicle reliably right now, Luc, so maybe we should wait until the morning sickness dies down. But I'll keep in mind that you told me not to dare."

"God." He was going to break this damn showerhead. "Summer, please. God. Just—tighter, all right? Faster. Just let me—finish off." *Because as soon as you do, I have plans for you.*

She laughed again, a little sound that whipped all through him. He was the one who was in control. Sure, they had played a little at other things since they got married, but never for long. He always flipped it. He'd never let her drive him to the breaking point before he took back that control and made sure she at least broke at the same time as he did, if not before. "I like this," she murmured, her voice far too light, far too pleased with herself for how crazy she was driving him. "This is fun."

Fun. "Summer," he said between gritted teeth.

"Oh, you poor baby," she cooed, starting to slide her hand back and forth in a steady rhythm. "Is that better?"

"*Yes.*"

"A lot better?" she murmured into his back. She shifted, dragging her breasts against his skin, which

104

shot something fierce all through him. Oh, so she wanted texture, too. *Just you wait, soleil. I'll give you some texture on your breasts. Two more minutes.*

Yeah, right. If he lasted two full minutes, it would be a miracle even of his control.

"Or would it be even better like this?" Her hand tightened, moving faster.

He groaned, wild. He hated that wildness in him. Yet he wasn't going to stop her. He wasn't going to turn around. "*Yes,*" he whispered into the muscles of his arm.

"But what if I wanted to take my time, Luc?" Her hand slowed down. "You know how I like lots of petting. What if I wanted to just pet you all over your back for the longest time? You have such a gorgeous back." She rubbed her face against it.

"Summer. *Some other time.*"

She laughed and bit him again, sharp and fierce. He thrust into her hand, and thrust again, and nearly wrenched that showerhead off the wall.

"Just tell me fast or slow," she whispered, as her hand moved. "You don't have to use words. I'll accept grunts and groans."

He wasn't a *savage*. "Tighter," he managed between his teeth. That sounded like a grunt, didn't it?

And then a hiss of a groan into his arm as she obeyed.

"God, this makes me happy," she said out loud, wonderingly, just before she cupped his balls again with her other hand, pressed her hips into his buttocks and her breasts into his back as hard as she could, and made him come.

Chapter 15

L uc hung exhausted from the showerhead, the water dripping down his body like sweat. But it was water, washing him clean again. That wild, wild creature he carried inside him eased now, at peace and a little smug, while his brain tried to recoup its power over his body. Over his heart. Oh, she was so going to pay.

That wild, satisfied part of him wanted nothing so much as to go to sleep, with her trapped under his arm, but his brain had long experience of driving him past any level of fatigue.

He turned, pain lancing through his hands as he finally loosed his grip on the showerhead. "Happy?" he challenged, intentions twining through his voice, so wicked he could taste them.

Her face startled him. Because she did look happy. Not even smug herself, just luminous with delight and relief, hair dampened to dark gold that smeared across her face, blue eyes sparkling and soft all at once. "Yes," she whispered, lifting her arms to curl her hands over his shoulders, snuggling her wet body into his.

He lifted her up in his arms, grabbing a fistful of towels off the rack as he carried her out of the bathroom. "How do you feel?"

She shrugged, moving one hand as if it searched for words. "Delicious," she finally decided, her eyes brimming with a hint of mischief but mostly just that happiness. It was an extraordinary thing to try to digest, that she could look so happy because she had made him come.

Was it at all possible he should—loosen up a bit? Relax his need for control? Trust her with him?

Shit, didn't he already do that? Was that, too, still a work in progress?

He liked making her come, too, but he wasn't sure he would quite define what he felt in those moments as happiness. It was fiercer and harder and more possessive. More animal, more hungry.

Well, we'll just have to work on your hunger levels, won't we, soleil? He didn't like being the only animal in the room.

He tossed towels onto the bed and set her onto them, pulling and tugging ostensibly to get them smoothed out under her—and then wrapping them suddenly around her body, a snug double-wrap that trapped her arms, the ends tucked under her body. She could wriggle free, but it would take her a while.

"Luc." She protested, but she was laughing.

Laughing. As much as he liked her laughter, there were moments when a man would far rather make a woman scream.

"Let me know if you need anything," he murmured, pushing her legs apart. Like, if she got suddenly sick again, it would be good if he didn't *miss that signal* this time around.

"Luc." It was a pretend protest. He knew those, very well. Her eyes had widened, and her sex—oh, yes, he could see how hot and wet she was for him. So she really had enjoyed that game. In more ways than one.

He slid his hand against her, enjoying how easily and deeply he could rub, how the lips of her sex were already parted and lush for him. She drew a breath and tried to wriggle her arms free. He grinned at her, feeling astonishingly light now that his own arousal no longer drove him so ruthlessly. It wasn't, actually, an experience he had ever had. He *always* made sure she came first, and often several times. It was a very strange thing to realize that they were married, and she was going to have his baby, and until a few minutes ago in

107

the shower he had never physically yielded himself to her before. Never just let her have control.

And that yielding of control had cost him so much he meant to recoup triple payback right now.

"I can see why you thought this was fun," he told her, delving into her a little, watching her face as he gently pinched folds of her flesh and rubbed them apart again.

She wet her lips, the laughter dissolving off her face as her hips lifted. "Luc."

"I always did love making you say my name." His fingers drifted deeper, slid the whole length of her wet, wet crease. Circled around her clitoris but didn't touch it, because—she had started that game.

"Luc." She lifted to him, trying to get his hand to the spot she wanted.

He laughed, his own arousal building lazily, no real pressure. Damn, this *was* fun. He didn't think they'd had fun together since they'd opened the new restaurant. Just relaxed, lazy, happy, sexy *fun*.

I love you.

"You have a very pretty sex," he told her, running his fingers through the dark gold curls and toying with that lushness some more. *Toying.* Yes. *You're mine to play with. You're mine.*

"Luc," she protested again, half-laughing, even as her hips twisted, even as her eyes closed and more moisture slicked his fingers. "That can't possibly be pretty."

"Oh, it is. You know sometimes when you get dressed in the morning—when you don't realize I'm paying attention and I can see your sex all primmed up so tight and proper—it's all I can do not to pin you down on that bed and force it to get all lush and open for me again."

She shivered and twisted. And then her eyes opened and held his. "Why do you stop yourself?"

LAURA FLORAND

Because—control. Because he wasn't an animal. Because he—"Stop asking questions," he told her, rubbing her clitoris just delicately as his finger probed a long, slick way into her.

She gasped and moaned, her muscles clenching around him, her hips lifting. He leaned over her, coming closer and closer to her face, watching her eyes as his fingers dipped into her again, as his thumb played and teased. "Luc!" she gasped as his thumb danced away again.

He kissed her, lush and deep as his fingers in her body, taking his time, taking her over. She wriggled her arms up enough to clutch at the edge of the towel, preparatory to breaking free, and he pulled back enough, remembering what had happened the last time he had trapped her.

But she didn't look as if she was fighting with revulsion. Oh, no. Not at all. She was softened and desperate, as if his yielding to her in the shower had made her all ready to yield to him.

"I love you," he remembered to tell her out loud, not just in his head. She sometimes had trouble hearing it, when it was just in his head. Even when he was *showing* her. Showing her just like this, for example. He pushed her legs wider, studying her sex. *Damn*, he loved seeing her so hot and open.

"Luc." Her voice changed to a husky, delicious sound that just rubbed all over a man's skin, waking his arousal up again.

Oh, yes, beg me. He laughed, so much happiness built up inside him that it had to escape.

"It's not funny!" She twisted her hips.

Oh, she felt that, too? That vulnerability and frustration, as her need built and he could still laugh? His laugh deepened, a low, almost growling sound. "It's fun, though."

"Luc."

109

Wrong technique, soleil. I can keep doing this forever if you keep saying my name like that.

Except that his arousal was starting to grow more determined again, pushing at him to take her just like this, all wrapped up like a present for him. *No*, he told it sharply. *I have other plans first.*

"Now I want you to imagine that what's exploring all this hot, tight wetness"—he ran his fingers teasingly over her and then more slowly and deeply dragged them the other way as he lowered his head—"is my mouth." He blew a hot breath over her.

She tried to throw an arm up, maybe to hide her face as she often did when she was close to coming, but it got caught, still trapped in the towel.

"Oh, look." He braced her thighs apart with his forearms and knelt between her legs. "You don't have to use your imagination anymore."

Damn, it was fun, running through all the different tones of frustration and desperation and convulsive, shaking pleasure with which she could say his name.

I love you, he thought, as they fell asleep, still tangled in each other, the towel that had trapped her long since kicked to the floor. Everything about the entanglement of their satiated bodies eased him. No room left for nightmares in this bed. Only love.

We really are going to be so happy.

Chapter 16

S ummer woke up happy. Well, she woke up nauseated, but somewhere in there was happiness. Then she figured out, from the silence, that what had woken her was that tiny, carefully soft sound of the door shutting as Luc snuck out of the house, trying not to wake her, and her happiness wavered.

She rallied it. *Hey, Summer. Guess what? No matter what Luc or anyone else does, you know who you and this baby can count on? Yourself.*

So she hopped out of bed in a surge of energy, which sent her straight to the bathroom to hang over the toilet for five minutes. It was hard to keep your courage up when your day started like that and swung back to it at random but frequent intervals all day.

Still...*it's you or no one, Summer. Get on your feet.*

Roar.

Sorry, kid, she whispered, patting her belly, as she switched the Beethoven out for Katy Perry and Gloria Estefan. *We'll get back to Beethoven later.*

Anyway, seriously, how well could its auditory functions possibly be developed at the age of six weeks? She looked it up on the web, and...aww. It was over an inch long now! It looked so...weird and tiny and alien and scary. And cute.

Big bold titles on the Wikipedia page drew her eye: Weeks 1-3, Weeks 4-5, Weeks 6-8, MISCARRIAGE. Bolded extra big, jumping out at her.

Damn you, Wikipedia. Twenty-five percent of pregnancies failed in the first six weeks, eight percent after...

She shut the Wikipedia page and stood there a moment. Then she thrust her jaw out. *Yeah, well, fuck you, world! Eat your fucking heart out, wanting something to go wrong with my baby. It won't. I'll take care of her.*

Or of him.

(A little black-haired boy, not careful or wary at all, so sure he was loved he laughed with it. He got sulky and stomped his feet and got into trouble, because he knew the worst that could happen to him was he might get a time-out.)

Were time-outs okay punishment?

One thing at a time, Summer. You can figure that one out later.

She spread her print-outs of different baby swings around her on her desk, along with her bolded list of criteria. Then she looked up the phone number of the department of mechanical engineering at MIT. The name "Corey" was enough to get most department heads' time. Well, the department heads themselves could be kind of oblivious, but their deans usually understood how university bread was buttered.

But at the last second, she hesitated and searched through her contact list. Because she actually kind of knew someone who was an engineer in materials science, who had graduated from another top engineering school in the US, and who might have more personal contacts with people she could recommend.

"Hey, Patrick."

"Well, hello there, Miss Sunshine." Patrick's voice was warm, easy, with just a faint hint of wariness. They used to flirt with each other and now they were both in their happy ever afters, but *nobody* trusted Summer Corey to actually mean hers. And he was, after all, Luc's closest friend in the world, more than a friend, really. A brother. Almost literally a right arm that had been cut off. Summer had never had a best friend, but she liked to imagine it sometimes, and when she did, her heart hurt for Luc and Patrick now. "How are you doing?"

Had Luc told him? Summer hesitated, not sure she should be the one to break the news, when Luc was the one who was so close to him. "Not too bad, all things considered."

"Homesick?" he asked sympathetically.

Luc hadn't told him then? *Why* hadn't Luc told him? Was it that far down on his list of things he believed in and wanted to focus on?

"A little bit." She frowned into that vision of Luc, cut off from his best friend for her, seeming to handle everything so perfectly as he always did and yet maybe...at heart as lonely and uprooted as she was? "So when are you and Sarah coming to visit?"

A little silence. One of those moments when she hated using a phone, when she wanted to see the face of the person who wasn't speaking.

"It's really beautiful here in June," she said awkwardly.

"I had no idea you'd miss me so much," Patrick managed in that lazy, amused voice of his. But a question lurked under it.

"Oh, well, you know..." *Not me, you idiot.* Could she expose a weakness she wasn't even entirely sure Luc had? How much she thought he might be missing Patrick? "I mean, it's lovely here, and the house has plenty of room. We're always happy to have people to visit."

"Are you," Patrick said thoughtfully.

Summer sighed. "Well, anyway. Listen, Patrick, I was wondering if I could talk to Sarah."

***

"So we just pick the peaches?" Snatch them off the tree as if they were starving? Like a little kid might once have snatched abandoned food out of the trash? Bile rose in Luc's gorge, and he forced it down, but it was like

113

forcing down this great, huge glob of food only half-chewed because his stomach was so desperate for it.

"It's an abandoned orchard," Nico said easily, bending down to pick up a fallen peach. "Look at that. Fresh in the sun like that." He bit into it, and his eyes closed, all his senses sinking into that flavor in his mouth, that big-shouldered, stocky farmer's body of his lost in sensuality. "God, that's good."

Luc's mouth watered. But even that rubbed all his nerves backward. It was so exactly the same way his mouth had once watered as he watched other people enjoy the food he had to steal or beg for. Or just never got at all.

"Here." Nico picked a fruit off the tree and handed it to him, as if he knew Luc needed baby steps to this. Probably couldn't guess the reason, though. Luc had not worn jeans with holes.

And his T-shirt was Dior, too.

He bit into the peach, and—*merde*, yes, that was good. So good. The burst of pleasure in his mouth relaxed the muscles in his neck, and the shiver of release ran all through his body. He tilted his head back, gazing at the green leaves and the dangling gold-pink fruit.

"There you go," Nico said, in that damn *tone* of his that made Luc want to say *baa*. Possibly neigh, like a wild foal being coaxed. A wild foal. When he was quite visibly and obviously the most civilized person possible, damn it. He made a point of it. "I mean, doesn't it seem a shame to let all this go to waste? When there are people starving?"

It...did, actually. A flashing vision of a black-haired child gazing with craving at the half-eaten apple someone was about to toss in the trash. Sometimes he'd been able to taste someone else's apple from the far end of a Métro station.

Luc frowned and slowly stroked the fuzz of the peach, tracing a trickle of juice from his bite mark. "Are you trying to convert me or something?"

"Not exactly. But you know—sometimes I care about the star count. Think I'd like to prove to the world that *real food*, like this, is worth a star. I think I could make a difference that way. Make people think. But sometimes, I mean"—a shrug of burly shoulders—"I'd like to do something more accessible. You know? Or take a *day* a week or at least a day a month where we just cook out in the open for people. *Outside*. For everybody. For anybody. For Gypsies and field workers who could never afford our restaurant."

Luc shot Nico a glance. He didn't think his chef de cuisine knew Luc was half Roma, and since his other half was Tahitian, he didn't know if his origins were that obvious just from looking at him. Just some random black-haired, black-eyed exotic, that was him to most of the world. In Paris, he had actually very rarely had to step outside his milieu of high-end luxury where everyone knew exactly who he was and thought he was a god. But when he did, sometimes people guessed he might be Arab or Latin American or...actually, the way his country was changing and people were getting used to it, sometimes these days people just guessed he was French. Kind of weird, but...nice.

Still, Provence was handling the huge influx of immigrant and migrant populations since the European Union even worse than Paris did. If Luc wasn't careful how he dressed, people driving by these fields would assume he was an illegal migrant worker from Morocco or a "thieving Gypsy", maybe with the word "filthy" behind it somewhere in their thoughts, even if they didn't say it out loud.

He'd been there, after all. The black-haired, bronze-skinned *gitan* with holes in his clothes, invisible or despised, his stomach never, ever full. He'd heard himself called *sale gosse* because he crept too close to people with food in their hands and eyed that food too hungrily.

"We could probably get funding for doing something like that, so it wouldn't be at a loss," Nico said. "I mean, it would even be good publicity for you."

Luc thought wryly of his wife and her cousins. Yeah, he was pretty sure he could get funding. Hell, Summer would set up a foundation for him to blow dandelions if he asked her, but this...this was more his style, and hers. She would be into it, actually. She would be excited, and start doing that thing she did, asking all kinds of questions about what they wanted to accomplish and how they intended to get there, until they *knew*.

He remembered making éclairs for those islanders she loved so much, out on the picnic tables a step away from the beach. It had actually been one of the most beautiful moments of cooking in his entire life of three-star chef achievements. And Summer had looked at him as if he had hung the moon.

His lips eased into a smile. He stroked the fuzz again. Were babies' heads fuzzy? He'd heard them compared to peach fuzz. His thumb touched the dripping juice again. His smile deepened. Also that they leaked a lot of liquids.

"Are you even going to last with me any length of time to get something like that set up?" he asked Nico and reached up to pick his first peach. His hand curved around the fruit in the tree above him, and he paused, savoring something oddly powerful about the moment. He'd spent his whole life in Paris. Fruits arrived in his kitchen in flats, cradled carefully in plastic. Or he'd picked them up himself at four a.m. at the restaurateurs' market in Rungis. But here he could pick fruit out of a tree. He could plant a seed and watch it grow and from it feed his wife and baby. "Because I keep getting the impression you're going to ditch me soon for something more your style."

Nico gave him that *nah-I-could-watch-a-cute-lamb-for-hours* smile. "You're pretty interesting. Anyway, I tend to think of things in terms of five-year commitments."

"What, were you in the Legion étrangère or something?" Luc asked wryly.

Nico just smiled at him benignly and started to fill his basket with peaches. Luc found himself eyeing the edge of the other man's T-shirt sleeve to see if a *Honneur, Fidelité* tattoo appeared when it slid up those bulky biceps.

"Speaking of things that aren't anybody's business," Nico said easily, "how are you handling imminent fatherhood?"

Luc clutched too hard and bruised his peach. He, who never hurt *anything* fragile. He could handle things that most people could break by breathing too hard. "It's not imminent. Seven and a half more months."

"Ah," Nico said and laid a couple more peaches oh-so-carefully into his basket, so that never a bruise could touch them. "That well?"

Luc frowned at him.

"How about Summer? I haven't seen her around the restaurant as much. She feeling all right?"

Luc scowled at his peach. "The scents are getting to her. I guess it's—I think it's just normal." He slid a glance at the other chef. "I don't suppose you know anything about pregnant women?" After all, the man could probably birth baby lambs with no problem.

A tiny grin almost escaped Luc, as he imagined Summer's reaction if he compared her to a ewe: laughing, minatory, coming at him with a pretend threat to his person that was really just an excuse to touch him. *Damn,* he missed his wife.

Nico looked, briefly, rather darkly amused and just shook his head. "You want me to ask my cousins?"

Luc's grip tightened on the poor peach. No. He could handle this on his own. He had to. He'd never been able to count on anyone but himself. Well, and Patrick, and look where that had gotten him.

"You want me to handle picking these peaches for you, so you can go home and ask your wife?" Nico said.

"She might have some thoughts about pregnant women. Considering, you know, that she is one."

Yeah, but what if she told him that she couldn't handle it, that she was going to leave him, go back to her islands where she was happy? Luc ran his thumb over the peach again, and at the movement, his lungs eased enough that he could breathe. *You're part of that island happiness now, remember?* Their bodies sprawled together last night in their bed... "She'll like this," he said. "The peaches. I want to do it for her."

"Luc."

Luc looked up at the unwonted seriousness in Nico's tone. Nicolas held his eyes, this strong, intent gaze Luc hadn't realized that hazel was capable of. "I hear becoming a parent for the first time is one of those great challenges people hit in their lives. In some cultures, they throw parties, do all kinds of things to organize help for the new parents. So if you want me to pick some peaches for you, so you can give them to your wife and still have time to talk to her—it's okay to let me have your back on this one. You'll get my back for me on something later, right? That's how it works. It's picking peaches, Luc. Trust me, I've done worse."

Yeah, there was a lot of blood and guts on the savory side of the kitchen. Or—Luc slid a glance to that edge of a T-shirt where no tattoo showed at all—in the Foreign Legion.

"You're not actually going to reach out and scratch me behind the ears at some point, are you?" Luc asked, reaching for another peach.

"Nah." Nico assessed him head to toe, sidelong, and then smiled. "You're not tame enough yet. You might bite."

You know, it was official. No one capable of handling a top kitchen was actually sane.

Chapter 17

L uc found Summer from the music. Bemused, he tracked it to a room he hadn't even realized they were using.

Summer was...*merde*, she looked so cute. He leaned in the doorway, the pure, damn adorableness of it punching him in the stomach. She had her eyes closed, and she was bumping and grinding and punching the air. *ROAR!*

She tried to roar, too.

Oh, hell, that was so cute it was *hot*, it grabbed him right between the legs and tried to jerk him over to her, and he braced himself against the door jamb, because he had *not* come over here to take his wife against her—desk?—in a two-minute quickie.

She had a desk?

A huge calendar papered the length of a wall, pages of a great desk calendar torn out and taped side by side, up through March. A big star marked February 12, the date the baby was officially due. Around the star, a heart had been drawn in marker, and it looked as if Summer had traced over that heart again and again, maybe every time she paused in front of it.

A corkboard was full of papers and some photos of people who looked in their early twenties, with that characteristic American softness to their lips, as if they'd never learned to use their facial muscles in anything but a smile. He'd never seen them before, a diverse mix of people who didn't look any relation to each other or to Summer. More papers were strewn across the desk.

The phone in Summer's hand rang, and her eyes opened as she started to answer it—and then she saw Luc.

Her face just *lit.* "Luc?" she said wonderingly, as if he'd just shown up alive after he'd been declared MIA for years.

And before he could figure out how to digest that, she was across the room in a lunge of delight, her hands clasping behind his neck, the phone's new "Roar" ringtone continuing in one of them, ignored. "Hey!" she said happily, squeezing him. "You came to *see* me. What are you doing here? It can't be three yet, can it?" Sometimes he could take a couple of hours' break at three. He'd made a point of it that brief period they were in Paris, but starting the new restaurant here had completely swamped him, and she'd adapted to his inability to get away without complaint, coming instead to him.

She'd acted so completely compliant about it and yet—*this* much happiness and surprise because he had taken a fifteen-minute break and walked over from the restaurant?

"Hey," he said and wrapped his free arm around her, holding her in close. Her body felt so sweet and warm against his. *Right where her belly is pressed against me, that's where our baby is.* And he felt instantly guilty that his penis was right at that level. "I brought you something." He lifted his basket.

"*Peaches.*" She grabbed one, pausing just long enough to kiss her lips to its skin and close her eyes in anticipation.

He parted his lips to offer to peel it for her, but it was too late. Her teeth sank deep into it, in one luscious, hungry bite. The sound she made in her throat charged every erogenous zone in his body. He tried to angle his body a little so that his damn penis wouldn't poke his baby in the head.

"Oh, God, that tastes so good. I haven't managed to eat more than crackers all morning. This is *perfect.*" Summer licked the juice that was running down the skin.

Luc wet his own lips.

"Did Nico bring them in?" she asked.

"No, I—I picked them."

Her head drew back in surprise. "*You* did?"

He shrugged awkwardly. "Also I made you some ice pops. I put them in the freezer."

"Peach?" she asked hungrily.

His teeth tried very hard not to set. "Lime."

"Oh." Her face tried very hard not to fall.

He gazed down at her a moment. And then he lifted his hand and gently stroked her hair from her face. "I'll tell you what. Why don't I make you some in half a dozen flavors. If you want a dozen different ones, just let me know."

Her face softened. She rubbed her face against his fingers and then just nestled her head against his shoulder, still holding her half-eaten peach in one hand. "You still love me, then?"

"I—" God, it scared the hell out of him, how often he had to reassure her about that. What if one day he forgot, and she just slipped through his careless fingers? *You, of all people, have no excuse for ever having careless fingers.* But still...it would be nice to relax once in a while. "Summer. Can we just take that as a given? Please."

But he caught the way her expression drooped, even half hidden by his chest, the way her head bent. So apparently they couldn't.

She nodded, though, as if they could. Damn it, it would make his life so much easier if Summer wasn't such a compulsive liar about her feelings.

"*Soleil.* I'll always love you. No matter how terrible I am at proving it to you, it will always be true."

She drew a little breath of relief and sighed it out against his chest, nestling her face into him. It drove him absolutely crazy that she would be *relieved* to hear he still loved her. *When he had just told her the day before.* How could she be *that* insecure?

121

"Me, too," she whispered. "I'll always love you, too."

His heart started to beat very fast. God, to just *tell* him that, when she could take herself and their baby away from him so easily and leave him with nothing. It was cruel.

"Hey." She looked up at him. "I will."

"I know." He smiled down at her. Part of him knew. The ever-shrinking part of him that was sane. That said to the rest of him: *She's not your mother, you idiot. How can you be* that *insecure?*

She stroked his face. "I really will."

He smiled wryly. "Because I'm so lovable, right."

"Well, yes. Exactly." She leaned up onto her toes to kiss him.

Mmm, that was good. Arousal, already punched awake by her dance and her bite of that peach, surged more eagerly. He wanted to wrap her up and bury himself deep and never, ever let go, but...no. He was here to check on her. To talk, not have a quickie and run back to work.

She relaxed down out of the kiss, smiling up at him, still caressing his face. "And you're not terrible at proving you love me, Luc. I'm just, you know, a little screwed up, and also I think this pregnancy stuff must be making me hormonal."

He turned his face into her hand and held it to him as he kissed her wrist. "You're not terrible at proving it to me either, *soleil*. I just—well, likewise."

A flicker of a teasing smile. "You're hormonal?"

"I certainly feel as if I am," he said, heartfelt.

She laughed a little, her hand caressing. Her eyes grew searching but tender about it, careful. "So...are you okay?" she asked, which confused him. That was what he had come home in the middle of the day to ask her.

"Never better." Right at that particular second with her pressed against him, it was almost true. "You?"

She made a so-so gesture with her hand. "Yucky," she said ruefully. "Most of the time." She lifted her peach. "*Thank you.*"

He bent his head until he could slide his lips right next to her ear. The scent of her hair, that coconut and tiare scent of her, went straight to his head. His heart. His groin. "You go ahead and crave whatever you want," he breathed. "And I'll give it to you."

Summer's breath drew in, fast and soft. Her hips nestled against his, seeking different pressures.

Mmm.

God, he could so easily keep nudging her right back against that desk right now.

He did nudge her back, but just so he could prop her on the edge of it and set the basket of peaches down beside her. "Eat your peach, *soleil.*"

Yeah, he could sublimate. He could get off on that, just watching her sit there, with her legs spread a little so he could stand between them, eating that peach, licking that juice. Maybe he'd snatch just a little bite of it from her hand.

Arousal pressed in him again, hungry and sweet. She was his wife. He had all the time in the world with her. Their *lives.* He could tantalize himself now and linger over the idea until tonight.

Although if that was the case, why did he always, always feel as if he didn't have enough time?

You might want to think about finding time to talk about baby names with your wife.

"What are you up to?" He picked up one of the papers spread on the desk behind her to see it better. A baby swing. Another. Another. With all their reviews printed up, highlights through different remarks. His heart squeezed. Was Summer getting worried about getting the baby right, too? "Isn't it a little early to start shopping for swings?" Thirty-three more weeks, right? He could get the restaurant running a bit more smoothly first, and then they could hunt for baby gear together. The thought of it bemused him.

But Summer's expression stiffened, this little flash in her eyes as if he had hurt her somehow. What? "Why too early?"

"Well, I mean—" He opened a hand helplessly. He hadn't even gotten used to the idea that a baby was going to *come*, and she was already outfitting them? "I want to help."

The stiffness relaxed out of her expression, her eyes crinkling a little with pleasure. "You do?"

What? "Of course I do." It sounded...adorable. Fun. Vastly reassuring, to walk hand in hand with her through stores trying to figure out what a baby needed. As if they were in this together, building a solid future, as if it was all just normal and happy and hopeful. "I *really* do," he realized. His schedule rose up before him like a wall, a monster wall with hands that grew out of its stones and grabbed at him greedily. The restaurant. All the demands of perfection that lay between him and that moment shopping for a future with his wife.

The restaurant was their future, too, though, right? Or was it only his? But if he didn't make it the best in the world, how would his little girl know her daddy was worth anything? How would his wife?

He'd married a woman who had he-wasn't-sure-how-many million dollars in her own portfolio and was heir to one of the wealthiest self-made men in the world. How did he prove he was worth her, except with, well, his own worth? What he was good at?

"Well..." Summer started to smile a little bit, half-embarrassed, half-excited. "I kind of went a different direction."

He glanced from the sheets to the computer to the wall of a calendar that went through six weeks after the baby was due. "Ordering online?" He could sit in front of a computer and look over choices with her, too, couldn't he? He could take a *minute, merde*. Why had he found it easier to go gleaning with Nico than to sit down and talk baby names and swing choices with his wife?

Wait, why the name Sarah and a phone number there? Surely not his old intern, Patrick's fiancée, Sarah? It was a common name.

"I'm starting a company!" It burst out of Summer happily. She bounced off the desk, pointing to some of the photos on the corkboard. "Well, I'll be the venture capitalist for it. I couldn't find the right swing, I looked and looked, and I finally realized it still hadn't been *made* yet. And—I don't know, we're starting with swings, but these two at Caltech are already excited about other things parents might want. That perfect thing, with quality. But I want to make it affordable, you know? I mean—a real person's affordable. Not something you have to spend two thousand dollars on to get the right thing. These two, here, I recruited from an entrepreneurship program at Berkeley, so they're all very excited about this."

Luc stared at her as she almost *babbled*, gesturing excitedly to pictures and dates on the calendar— apparently the team was being flown over here next week, for example.

He started to grin, her energy both enthralling and reassuring. She was excited. Looking to *their* future.

Even if he hadn't known a thing about it.

"You know, you have a lot more of your father in you than you realize," he said admiringly.

Her face shut down that fast, as if he had slapped her.

Which—granted, maybe her father wasn't the best comparison for him to make, but... "The good part of him. His brains. His way of looking at the world and being able to get a project off the ground or turn a company around with a few savvy decisions."

Summer gave him a slightly stiff smile and nodded, shifting away to study her calendar. Her damn father. But it was true that she had his brilliant mind, and that she undervalued herself all the time. Thanks, of course, primarily to her damn father.

Maybe even thanks to people like Luc himself, her own husband, who even though he *knew* better, still tended to look at her and think how pretty she was, how sweet, how sexy, and forget to think about how smart and capable she was, too.

"Like you've helped me with the restaurant," he said, following her to put his hand on her shoulder. "I don't know what I'd do without you."

It was hard for him to say, to let her know that he really might not be able to make it without her, but the pleasure on her face was worth it. "Really?" she asked shyly.

"Oh, God, Summer...the accounts. When I try to do them—"

She lifted her hand to pet his hair back from his face, his misstep over her father forgiven and forgotten. "Don't do the accounts," she told him. "Just trust me on this. One accountant per set of account books. I'll let you know if I start embezzling."

He laughed, and the laughter felt so good, as if all of the stress and panic of the past few days might just be dissolving away, and...his gaze flicked over the calendar beyond her, and a note a few weeks out just slammed into him: *Manunui??*

His hand tightened so hard on her shoulder that Summer made a little sound and tried to jerk free.

And he didn't let her.

"Luc!" She pried at his fingers.

He forced them loose—only to press his hand against the calendar, walling her in. "Are you planning a trip?" He could barely hear his own voice. But it cut, coming out. Cut his throat, the edges of his too-tight lips.

"No, I decided to make the Caltech grads come to me," Summer said. "They'll love the trip to Provence, who wouldn't, in the middle of grad school, and I started thinking about how sick I might get on a plane flight..."

His finger tapped the name of her island once, hard. "What's this?"

"Oh." She looked from it to his face and back, her happiness faltering more and more. As if she knew something was wrong, but had no clue what. "I was hoping by then my stomach would be calmed down enough that I could make a trip to see everyone."

He couldn't even feel his own heart beating.

"I want to go *now*," she said wistfully, completely oblivious to his frozen heart, as if she didn't even care if she destroyed him, as if she wouldn't even *notice*. "But those sea planes make me sick even when I'm not pregnant. And let's not even talk about boat travel."

"*You can't go.*" The words sliced through the air.

Summer stared at him in confusion, fingering her throat as if he'd just sliced through that, too.

He scrambled for anything to keep her here. Her fears. The thing hidden on those tabs on her computer, the thing she was most afraid of. "You need to be near a doctor! What if something goes wrong?"

She gave a little gasp of breath and tried to step back. Her shoulders hit the calendar behind her, and he grabbed them.

"You know how high the chances are of something going wrong the first trimester! And you're so sick, Summer. What if that's a bad sign? What if you had a *miscarriage,* Summer? You *can't* go."

Her face went white. She stared at him, this thing rising in her eyes, as if he had just knifed her. Her hands went up to fold over her belly, as if that was where his knife had stabbed.

Her eyes were already damp with the rise of tears when they started to blaze. The force of the look shocked through him. They'd had a hard road to understand each other, when they first met, but he had never seen her look at him with this much rage, this much betrayal. Summer was *passive*-aggressive. She absorbed blows and hid their hurt under a smile, until so much rage built up in her that it exploded out destructively.

It was exploding out now.

"Go away." Her hands rose and slammed into his shoulders with all her force, trying to shove him back from her. "*You get away from me.*"

He didn't want to release her, oh, God, he didn't. But he realized suddenly how very hard his hands were gripping her shoulders. Shit. He jerked them away.

She slid fast along the wall away from him, holding his eyes as if she needed to be ready to dodge his next knife blow. "Don't you *talk* to me." The peach got in her way as she tried to reach for the sliding screen door out onto the terrace, and she *threw* it at him. It hit him in the shoulder. He didn't even try to catch it or avoid it. His reflexes had abandoned him.

She was abandoning him.

She had just *thrown* something at him. Fine, it wasn't something that could really hurt, but...the gesture hurt.

Her eyes blazed with rage and pain. As if he'd literally struck her, as if he'd destroyed something. "You go back to your restaurant, since that's all you care about anyway, and you *stay away from me.* Don't you *ever* talk to me again."

His heart beat so fast and hard it made him sick. He had to put a hand up to his chest to try to keep it from ripping out of his body in panic. "Summer—"

The screen stuck a little and she had to push it hard. He had just started forward instinctively to help her when she got it wide enough to slip her slim form through. She looked back at him as she got through the crack, with another surge of that wild, bitter rage as her hand came back to cover her belly protectively again: "*Fuck you.*"

"Summer—" He went after her, shoving the door wider, but she threw him another bitter look and took off on the path down the cliff to their little *calenque*, their sheltered beach.

He stopped on the terrace, gripping stone wall too thick even for his hands, but he found a grip on it anyway, dragging his fingers raw. Pain and fear and betrayal squeezed down on him until he felt compressed, as agonized as the minute speck of matter that contained all the universe just before it blew up. Even his breaths came short and tight, as if he had been locked in a space too small for his lungs to fill.

Everything struggled inside that tightness, too many things: Summer's happiness on her island; a childhood dragged through the Métro and sleeping in the streets, imagining a mother he had never known, who had abandoned him for her island happiness; the look on Summer's face when he had said, when he had said—

How could he have said that to her? Even to protect himself, even to keep her trapped here, how could he have said that?

He pulled out his phone suddenly and sent three texts. Patrick. Sylvain. Dom. *I need your help.*

Chapter 18

S ummer wrote, "10 am: Maia, Skype" on Tuesday on her calendar, her whole arm heavy. It was Sunday morning, the day Luc could take off, they day they could talk.

Except she wasn't talking to him. He'd tried to follow her to the beach to tell her he was sorry, and she'd just dived into the water in her underthings, swimming. She could swim around an entire island when she was in the mood. In the South Pacific, she and some of the other islanders used to do that kind of thing for fun. Or just because, particularly on an island, sometimes you just needed to leave behind the world that trapped you and swim and swim.

By the time she'd come back out, Luc had given up, sitting on the beach by her abandoned clothes with his arms locked around his knees, watching her, waiting, not trying to talk again in case she dived right back into the water. That night, she'd slept in the guest bedroom. Luc, intense and pale, hadn't argued with that either. He'd just dumped a stack of thick towels on her wet body and stood there looking at her a moment, his fists clenching and unclenching, his face in that honed, forged-in-the-fires-of-creation expression of his, and then walked out and left her alone.

Fuck you, Luc.

I'm all alone here. I came here for you. You're the only person in the world I thought I could trust to fight for this baby, to be on our side, and you, and you...

She swallowed against the burn in her throat. *If I'm all this baby has, then I'll damn well do a good job on my own.*

The scent of the peaches, still in a basket on her desk from the day before, forced their scent on her, ever thicker and sweeter, soon to be rotten and miasmic if she left them.

Voices burst in on her out of nowhere, like a car wreck, this pile of excited feminine sounds.

"There's the mama!"

"I can't believe you didn't tell me!"

Summer turned, completely confused, as her cousins swept in on her. Cade and Jaime, Cade in jeans but otherwise looking as efficiently put together as always, her fine, straight, light brown hair twisted on top of her head, and Jaime with that red-caramel hair in a sweeping reverse wedge cut that looked surprisingly good on her. Summer always associated Jaime with ponytails and braids, or she had until Jaime's hair had to be cut so short after her...accident. But the steeply angled sweep of her hair past her jawline gave her a surprisingly sophisticated prettiness, highlighting the Audrey Hepburn bones of her face, all dusted over with freckles as if the sun hadn't been able to stop kissing her and had left its marks over every single inch of her skin.

The sun being probably exactly like Dom, Summer thought with an amusement that turned into wistfulness. Luc used to feel that way about her, wanting to kiss her all over. Maybe she shouldn't be in here wantonly destroying that urge of his out of her own hurt and fear.

"Summer!" Cade *hugged* her, throwing Summer completely off-balance. She knew she'd hugged Cade once, in a quest for asylum, but...were they going to make a habit out of physical affection? Summer had always been desperate for more of it, and the happy Corey sisters had never bothered with it, too secure to need it, too busy with their own spats to want to get that mushy.

Jaime threw an arm over her shoulders and gave them a loose squeeze, as if she knew a full-blown hug might be a bit much, the first time around. "Look at you," Jaime said affectionately. "A *mama*. You're going to be the first of us!"

Summer struggled with one of those stupid, sudden threats of tears. Something about the word *mama,* or the hugs, or the friendly admiration in the sisters' tones got to her so deeply.

"Yeah, you're the guinea pig," Cade told her. "I expect you to get this all figured out for us, so we'll know what to do when it's our turn."

Summer stared at her in-charge-of-the-world cousin, completely thrown. Summer was the leader? She was the one her cousins were going to look up to?

But, of course: *They don't have a mother to help them with this at all. Their mother* died.

Julie Corey. Summer had loved Julie Corey so much, and her death when Summer was twelve had been a brutal blow. But how much worse for her own daughters, of course, than for the second cousin who tried to slip in and just pretend she was Julie Corey's daughter whenever she could.

"What's this?" Cade's business eye was already drawn to the calendar and the pin-ups of swing designs, probably able to guess at least half the answer to her question just from the glance.

"Well...I couldn't find the right swing," Summer admitted. "So now I'm going to fund a start-up."

Cade laughed out loud. "You go!" She held up her hand, and it took Summer a blank second to realize she was being given a high five. Jaime gave her one, too. The impact on her palm tingled. Felt...warm. "I told you she would figure it out for us," Cade told Jaime.

Really? Cade hadn't assumed Summer would screw it all up?

"Wait, what—how do you even know? What are you doing here?" Had her *mother* told them?

"Well, not because you told us, that's for sure," Jaime said, with only half-kidding severity. "You know, I can read texts if you don't want to bother to call."

"Luc." Cade laughed and rolled her eyes.

"Luc called you? Last night?" After their fight?

"Are you kidding me? He's called pretty much every day since you learned it. Sylvain can't stop laughing."

What?

"It's hilarious." Cade grinned.

"Dom's a little bit pissed," Jaime mentioned. "Since he and Luc were the ones who actually worked together in a kitchen back when they were starting out. His feelings are hurt Luc would call Sylvain instead of him." Then Jaime grinned, too. "It's pretty cute. He gets all grumpy and go-to-hell about it. But if you could just slip a word in Luc's ear that it might be nice to call Dom a time or two, too, I'd appreciate it."

"Luc keeps calling you?"

"Yeah, I should probably just buy up the entire contents of the American store in Paris and ship it down here to you to save on trips, but then I would miss out on all the fun of hearing him try to act as if he's not in the least desperate and confused." Cade started laughing again.

Jaime looked disgruntled. "See? I don't understand why Cade gets all the fun."

Cade just laughed again. "Umm...how do you think Dom would react if some other hot chef started calling you every day?"

Jaime scrunched up her face as she considered. Then she shook her head. "Yeah, that couldn't end well."

"What does he call about?" Summer asked blankly.

"Oh, my God. Pickles." Cade was dissolving into chortles. "Peanut butter. Whatever he thinks you might be able to eat. The man has gone off the deep end. It's pretty adorable, actually. Especially when he starts hinting about how lovely Provence is this time of year."

"Hinting about...Luc invited you two down here? When? Last night?"

"The first time was a few days ago." Cade grinned again. "I have the impression he needs a little moral support."

"Hey," Jaime said, before Summer could quite decipher all of this. She was looking at Summer's notes on the calendar and desk. "I know some women in Côte d'Ivoire who were designing the most perfect baby sling," Jaime said. "They were just doing it as a small business—micro-funded, you know—but if you're interested in doing more products than swings, I could put you in touch. Their slings were really pretty. All these bright colors."

"I'd invest in that," Cade said. "Especially if you're guiding the entrepreneurs, Summer. You'd make sure they have their heads screwed on straight, when it comes down to actual business."

"You would?"

"It would be cool," Jaime said. "Particularly if it can help support small businesses like that sling one. Micro-funding for women entrepreneurs in developing countries. I'd sit on the board. Hey, and did you think about devoting a part of the profits to providing supplies and medical care to low-income moms or teenagers in at-risk pregnancies?"

Summer blinked. The project expanded in her vision, linking to other people, becoming more and more...*implicated.* Not an island. Not alone.

"Count me in." Cade pushed open the glass doors to step out onto the terrace that ran the length of the house. "Wow, your view. Beautiful." Cade stopped at the wall and gazed down the herb-dotted cliff to the Mediterranean, then tossed Summer a smile over her shoulder. "Not *too* big a change from your island, then?"

As much as Summer loved the sea and scents of Manunui, the people were what she missed the most. And the safety from the judgment of the whole rest of the world.

"*Magnifique*," came a male voice from farther down the terrace. Sylvain stepped out through the glass doors from the kitchen, tall and physical and graceful, a poet crossed with an athlete. In some ways he reminded Summer a little bit of Luc—both roughly of a height, both black-haired, both with that passionate intensity—but Sylvain was so much more relaxed and amused in his skin. Luc worked so damn hard to fit right in his own. So focused on making everything about himself perfect, all the time.

Sometimes, once in a rare, rare while, Summer managed to convince him for the space of a nap in a hammock or a lazy afternoon that he was still perfect to her, even when he stopped trying.

"I wouldn't mind working in a kitchen with *this* view," Sylvain added as big, dark Dominique Richard followed him out. Dom brought that rough suggestion of danger to the terrace, but Summer was more comfortable around him these days than she once had been. Mostly because he seemed to like her a lot more these days. Ever since he and Jaime had spent a week on the island for Luc and Summer's wedding, his attitude toward her had shifted to this rough-edged, casual affection.

Summer loved it. She'd always had a really huge weakness for being liked.

Luc stepped out onto the terrace after the other two men and looked at her immediately, quick, intense, searching. His face tightened a little at whatever he saw, and he slipped his hands into his pockets and went with Dom and Sylvain to the wall to look at the view.

"Oh, before I forget." Cade pulled a big jar of peanut butter out of her purse—the Corey brand from Summer's childhood visits to her cousins.

"*Merde*, Cade." Down the terrace, Sylvain made a dramatic show of wincing and holding up a cross to ward off the devil. "Couldn't you have waited until I was out of sight?"

Big, bad Dom rolled his eyes and heaved a sigh. No matter what Sylvain reacted to, Dom pretty much had to treat it like a ridiculous reaction. That was just the way those two fit together.

"Luc really wanted peanut butter?" Summer glanced toward him involuntarily.

His hands were still in his pockets, the way they always were when he struggled with too much emotion and didn't have a dessert outlet for it. His eyes held hers as soon as she gave them the chance, pleading and pushing all at once. *I'm sorry.*

Her breath tightened, and she covered her belly to protect it again from his hurt.

"Apparently it might help you with your nausea." Cade grinned and held out the peanut butter. "You want some?"

"Umm...maybe in a little bit." Summer couldn't even conceive of wanting peanut butter, not with her stupid stomach, but she took the jar politely and snuck a glance at Luc again. He hadn't looked away. He leaned back against the terrace wall with the other two as if he was relaxed, but there wasn't a relaxed line in his body. Even at the best of times, that man was terrible at relaxation.

He needed her for it. If he didn't have her, he'd tighten and tighten himself, like a guitar string that was too stubborn to snap. Titanium that would break the tuning pegs, break even the fingers twisting them, before he would break himself.

Her heart ached again, and her free hand kneaded her belly nervously. *Why did you say that to me?*

That ugly, terrible thing.

I trusted you with the most fragile, precious thing about me, and you struck at it to save yourself.

"I still can't believe you didn't tell us yourself!" Jaime exclaimed. "If Luc hadn't needed pickles and peanut butter, we still wouldn't know. We've been *waiting* for you to crack and call us yourself, so we could pretend to be surprised. What's the fun in having a baby all alone?"

136

Well...well...good point. But when would Summer have gotten the courage to reach out to her cousins and risk more reactions like her mother's?

Or Luc's.

"Well, it's early yet," she tried. *Apparently I'm not supposed to tell anybody at all yet. So if something does go wrong I can be all alone with it, I guess. Wouldn't, after all, want to cling to others during a terrible time and burden them with...me.*

"*You* knew," Jaime argued. "Me knowing was just a phone call away."

"Excuse me?" Cade adopted that calm superiority she did so well. "I'm the oldest. She should have called me."

"You should have called me," Jaime told Summer. "So as not to expose your baby to noted chocolate felons." Cade's reputation as a chocolate thief was going to follow her forever. "But either way, you should have called one of us."

"They say not to start announcing it until after the first three months." Summer looked at Luc again, a sharp, hard glance, shards of glass cast across the terrace, glinting in the light. His lips pressed in that merciless self-control of his, but his eyes held that wild, intense mix of pleading for forgiveness and accusation. *I'm sorry. I'm sorry.* And, *How could you?*

She bent her head.

"Oops," Cade said wryly, her own blue eyes laughing, in complete innocence of any concerns about a first trimester. "Well, the cat's out of *that* bag. What with all those calls for pickles."

"So it's true about the cravings?" Jaime asked curiously. "You hear rumors, but—" She waved a hand at the peanut butter in Summer's hand.

"Having Luc Leroi hunting for American pickles and *peanut butter* makes it really hit home," Sylvain supplied, amused.

"There is nothing wrong with peanut butter, Sylvain," Cade told him, with steely patience.

Sylvain made a little sound of compressed hilarity and raised his eyebrows innocently at his wife's look. "No, of course not, *chérie*," he said with such patent insincerity that Cade poked him. He caught her poking finger and rubbed his thumb over the tip of it, gentle, subtle, possessive.

Summer glanced again at Luc, the distance between them this ache in her throat. He stared back at her a moment and then left the terrace abruptly.

***

In the kitchen, Luc stood alone in front of the open freezer, still for a moment, then forcing himself to pull out the ice pops. What would she like this time? Probably any choice would be wrong. Lime, he guessed wildly, but mostly even that choice was for selfish reasons. Mostly it was because he wanted back that moment when she had said, *Mmm, because it smells like you.*

He wanted to be *mmm* again. He wanted...anything, really.

But he wanted to cut her passport into tiny ribbons, too. And he had barely enough control over that desire not to actually do it. She kept it in their safe. He knew right where it was. She trusted him with it. It had never occurred to her that she couldn't.

It should never have occurred to him. And yet he had had to stop himself from attacking it with a pair of kitchen shears every single second of the past twenty-four hours.

He set the lime ice pop on a tray, along with a baguette and a selection of glasses and options for drinks, carrying it out for their guests. It was rude to serve his own wife before their guests, but he brought her the ice pop first anyway.

She just barely glanced at him. But he got to touch her hand very gently when he put the ice pop in it. *I'm sorry. I didn't mean to hold on to you so tightly that I hurt you.*

And: *Don't disappear on me. Please don't. Please don't. I'll get better at this. Please stay.*

"Oh, is Luc making you Popsicles?" Cade exclaimed and gave Luc the fondest smile he'd gotten since he managed to alienate his own wife. "That's so sweet."

"Eating has been a little tricky," Summer admitted to her cousins, rubbing her belly. But she slipped the ice pop into her mouth, and something about her relaxed when she did. Her eyes closed, and she took a deep breath.

So some tiny part of Luc relaxed, too.

Jaime caught Summer's hand and lifted it to study her stomach. "You can't even tell yet!" she exclaimed, disappointed. "When does it start showing?"

"Not for a few more weeks, I think." Summer nodded to the pregnancy book she had left by the hammock on the terrace. Luc had been paging through it that morning, the morning off he had meant to spend with his wife. Reading what was happening to her body was the closest he could come.

"Oh, they have books," Cade said with relief. Behind her, out of her line of sight, Sylvain studied his wife very curiously, eyes alert. "I suppose there are some kind of classes you can take, too?"

"I hope so," Summer said wryly. "I only just found out for sure last week, about the same time I started feeling so sick."

"Is the morning sickness lousy?" Jaime made a face. "Is it true what they say, that you get sick *every* morning?"

"It's more like all the time." Summer winced, probably battling nausea right this second. Luc opened the damn peanut butter jar, tore off a hunk of baguette, and spread it with peanut butter, handing it to her.

Summer looked at him as if he had descended from another planet. *Tombé de la lune.* Fresh fallen into her world, disoriented and confused, and desperate to be accepted into it.

She nibbled a bit of the bread, then sucked again on her ice pop.

Cade grimaced sympathetically. "Apparently with me and Jaime, our own mom couldn't stand chocolate."

Sylvain jerked upright.

"She couldn't even stand the *smell* of it," Cade said. "And you know the whole town of Corey smells of it, right? She had to spend the entire first trimester at our beach house, both times."

Sylvain stared at Cade, appalled. Nice to know Luc wasn't the only one thrown for a loop by the ramifications of his wife's pregnancy. That cocky bastard Sylvain couldn't even handle an imagined one.

"So you weren't scared at all?" Jaime asked curiously.

"I wasn't, actually," Summer said softly. "I was really excited." After a second, she admitted more softly still: "Now I'm scared."

Luc's fingers flexed in uneasy fists. A vision of the night she had told him, him leaning back against the alley wall, trying to be strong. He'd failed her.

"Yeah, I bet," Cade said wonderingly. She reached out to touch Summer's belly. Cade, whom no one would have described as touchy-feely. "Does it feel strange? To have someone growing inside you?"

Luc blinked. Wasn't it just—natural? It sounded disturbing to *him*, but didn't women just handle that idea as part of who they were?

"*Yes.*" Summer kneaded her belly some more. "Sometimes you feel like one of those women in bad movies who has been possessed by an alien. And then you feel guilty, because it's your baby."

He'd never known she thought that way. Why hadn't she told him? It was funny and sweet and understandable all at once, and he would have kind of liked to put his cheek against her belly at night and tease her about their little alien until she was laughing instead of worried.

When would she have told you? When have you relaxed and let her?

Merde, when have you put your cheek against her belly and teased and believed in her?

God, all the ways she tried to support him every day. Summer Corey, one of the wealthiest heirs on the planet, folding his napkins and joking with the staff while she helped. The utter confidence she gave him that he could accomplish anything he set out to do.

What would it feel like, if he didn't have that?

Maybe she needs you to believe in her, too.

She even said so once. "If you can trust me, I can trust you. And if not, it all falls apart."

Jaime laughed. "I remember one of the execs at Corey did that 3D ultrasound, and when she was showing the pictures, it was all I could do not to say it looked like a goblin. Fortunately, it turned out to be a cute little baby girl."

"When will you know if it's a boy or a girl?" Cade asked. "You're going to find out, aren't you?"

Were they going to find out? Would it be more fun to know or not? But Summer was already nodding eagerly. When she hadn't even talked to him about it.

Well, it was her body, of course, but...sometimes she let him have a say in what happened to her body. Sometimes she liked letting him have *all* the say. Granted, it wasn't quite the same context, but...

When would she have talked with you?

He frowned and walked back over to the terrace wall, to lean against it between Dom and Sylvain. The two men always left a sizable space between themselves, which was kind of funny, considering how they always seemed to be on the same side of the room. Together against the world, as long as they didn't have to admit it.

He missed Patrick so badly it hurt his heart. People latched onto your heart that way. And as soon as they had sunk their fingers in deep, they ripped out a great chunk and walked off with it, leaving what was left of the heart bleeding and broken. He looked at Summer again, at that baffled, hungry smile that was starting to relax her face as her cousins kept asking her fascinated questions.

"How did you do it?" Dom asked suddenly, low.

"Get my wife pregnant?" Luc asked dryly, because he had no idea how to answer the real question. He'd believed in her. In them. That was how he had done it. He'd believed she wouldn't walk away with a chunk of his torn-to-pieces heart.

He'd believed that against all possible evidence from every single other important relationship he had ever had in his life.

Well, he'd *tried* to believe it. He'd meant to.

"Get up the courage." Dom looked down at one of his big, scarred hands, curled around the stone of the terrace wall. "You weren't scared out of your mind?"

"I had this vision." It bloomed in him again, beautiful: black-haired kids running up to greet him when he got home, chasing each other through lavender as he and Summer walked hand in hand behind them. "It was perfect." He looked at Summer again, her smile growing stronger and truer the more she answered eager questions. "Now I'm scared," he admitted softly.

Just like her.

"I wondered. I mean, it's not as if your own dad was—" Dom broke off.

Thank you. I know. And he was pretty sure Dom's own father was even worse. Luc's father had slapped him a few times, grabbed him too hard in a temper, used him to beg for money in the Métro and the streets, and

142

blamed him when they didn't have enough, and eventually he'd lost him to the foster care system, but...well...he'd *tried*. Luc was pretty sure Marko had and still did genuinely love him, as best he could.

It was terrifying. Because if that was the best his own father could do, *merde*...

"You'll do perfectly," Dom said abruptly, firmly. "You always get everything perfect."

"I practice," Luc said, driven. "And you can't practice on your *kids*. You've only got one chance."

I guess we should have had another kid so we could have gotten that one right, Summer's father Sam Corey had once said, and it had been all Luc could do not to punch him.

"No, you don't." On Luc's left, Sylvain thrust away from the wall, sounding exasperated.

Luc and Dom both looked at him.

Sylvain flung out his hands. "You think my father never screwed up with me? You think *I* never screwed up with him? You don't get only one chance, for God's sake. You get five million chances, second after second every day. You don't have to get every single one of them perfect. *Merde.* It's not *chocolate.*"

The last word knocked a laugh out of Luc, his whole body relaxing with it. "So as long as it's not chocolate, it's okay to mess it up?"

"Well, *yes*," Sylvain said impatiently. "It's not the same thing at all." He considered, moving his hands the way he often did, as if he had to imagine textures in order to process his own words. They all did that, actually. "The only way I could get Cade and me perfect, all the time," he said finally, "is if I turned her into this thing. Turned *us* into a thing. Chocolate. She wouldn't let me, of course. But if I *tried*—can't you see how much harm I would do?"

Summer had several times firmly stopped Luc from treating her like a thing. Like his product to get right.

She called him on it immediately when she caught him at it, these days with an amused *Luc!*

"You mean, if I try to get everything right, *that* will screw things up, too?"

"Exactly." Sylvain gave him a wry, sympathetic look. "Sorry, Luc."

"Then how the hell do I get everything right?" Luc asked between his teeth.

"You don't. You have to learn to live with *screwing up.*"

Luc just stared at him.

"I think you have to learn to relax," Sylvain said, with unusual caution, as if he realized he was telling Luc to grow three heads. After a second, with a wry smile, he offered Luc his glass of pastis.

"No, thank you," Luc said sternly, pushing the alcohol away. If he had to learn how to relax, he sure as hell needed to keep his control.

Chapter 19

66 Men. Seriously." Cade paused in front of a shop window in the medieval part of the beautiful hill town of Sainte-Mère—Summer having wanted to share a bit of the region with them—and looked back at the husbands and fiancé who had completely failed to keep up with them. The men had stopped by the wall of the terrace at the top of the town, with the *boules* court just behind them, and stood in a loose circle, framed by the Alps and the sea. Snow clung to the highest peaks, this surreally beautiful white-blue vision when seen from the heated stone and jasmine of the town.

But instead of looking at the view, all three men were focused on their cell phones.

"You'd think they could at least make the effort to talk to each other," Cade said, exasperated.

"Don't start asking Dom and Sylvain to talk to each other this early in the day," Jaime said, amused. "They've got a whole weekend to get through without a fight." Sunday and Monday or Monday and Tuesday counted as weekends for anyone in the restaurant business.

Cade grinned at Summer. "They never do really get in a fight, don't worry. It's kind of hilarious how much they like each other but can't admit it. And don't you dare tell Sylvain I let anyone know he likes Dominique."

"Yes, it would be very awkward for everyone," Jaime agreed. "I can't tell you how many family dinners would be ruined if those two had to admit they get along. Next thing you know, Dad might have to admit he kind of respects them, and God knows where it could all end."

Summer bit back a grin at the image of Mack Corey, billionaire bulldozer, trying to handle the two equally arrogant men who had won his daughters. Damn it, the amount of times she'd gnawed her own heart out wishing she'd been born to Jaime and Cade's parents instead of her own. But maybe Mack would have made mincemeat out of Summer the same way his cousin Sam had. Maybe Jaime and Cade were just made of stronger stuff.

Summer looked at her husband in the distance. Luc had that kind of rapport with Patrick, like Sylvain and Dominique. No, much stronger. The two had pretended to drive each other crazy, while *always* having each other's backs. Luc had lost him, when he came to the south of France for her. Patrick had chosen to follow his own dream.

Luc and Summer, together against the world.

So beautiful and romantic in concept, and so heartbreaking in fact.

"This whole not knowing the sex business is annoying," Cade stated, examining a storefront gracefully positioned near an old stone *abreuvoir,* a watering trough. "You can't even start buying cute clothes yet. And look at that little dress."

The little galleries and boutiques catered to the wealthy crowd who came up from the yachts moored at Cannes, and this particular one featured high-end, one-of-a-kind children's clothes, complete with options for hand-tailoring. A couple passed them, a big brown-haired man with his hand around a smaller blond woman's, strolling under an arch at one side of the *place* and up a cobblestone street lined with shops and houses framed with bougainvillea and ivy and jasmine, red geraniums in pots on the balconies. Jasmine scented everything.

Jaime slid her older sister a bemused look, one eyebrow going up a little bit. "You have a weakness for cute baby girl clothes?"

Cade gave her a dirty look with no real heat in it—Summer felt that old shaft of jealousy at the Corey sense of sisterhood, wondering if Luc was feeling something of the same thing toward Sylvain and Dom—and switched her attention to some soft leather booties. "Now these would be cute on either sex. You know what I like about France?"

"Sylvain," Jaime supplied, her lips twitching.

Another of those sisterly, pseudo-annoyed glances as Cade kept on going. "All the *colors* in little girl clothes. Red. Blue."

"Gray," Jaime said thoughtfully, eyeing a tiny outfit that was, indeed, gray. "Black. It's a different take, I'll grant you."

The three women grinned at each other as, without even finishing the articulation, they all got a vision of a little French toddler sleeked out in black and looking infinitely classy.

"Your mom used to put you in that kind of thing," Cade remembered, to Summer. "Our mom mostly stuck us in play clothes. I remember you showing up in the prettiest heels one time, when you were, what, six? Meanwhile, *my* dad absolutely put his foot down. I think I was sixteen before I got to wear heels. And then he let Jaime when she was fourteen, which was completely unfair."

"I rebelled better than you," Jaime retorted. "It's not my fault it was so easy to get you to toe the line."

"Which do you think you'll do?" Cade asked Summer, ignoring her sister with that ease that always made Summer just want to squeeze her way into their lives and be a sister, too. "If you have a little girl, will it be play clothes or pretty dresses?"

A little black-haired girl rose in her head so vividly her heart tightened with pleasure and anxiety and hope. If only Summer could do everything right, that little girl was going to be so *beautiful.* Summer tilted her head, considering that little girl carefully. "Both, I think. Whichever she's in the mood for at the time." It would be okay if she tore her pretty dresses because she decided she wanted to play. Summer wouldn't say she was too spoiled to respect her things. It had always been more important to her own father to respect things more than people. She'd gotten denied dessert many, many times because she'd torn the lace on a dress playing or lost an expensive bracelet off a toddler wrist.

Or given her bracelet away to a boy she met on the playground. A nine-year-old black-haired boy who lifted her six-year-old self up to reach the monkey bars, and showed off for her, and acted as if she was a fairy princess.

She turned enough to look at Luc, engrossed in his phone while Sylvain gestured large and Gallic with his own phone in one hand and Dom shook his head.

A little smile eased her mouth, out of the blue. One thing was sure, no matter how much their little girl tore her pretty dress, her daddy would never deny her dessert.

Her heart softened at the vision of him, making all those beautiful creations for her, making them for some little girl or boy, this great hunger in him for them to be hungry for him. If it was true that whimsical thing she liked to believe, that he was the young dark-haired boy she had met once on a playground in Paris, then even as a little boy playing on the playground, determined to impress the little girl he'd met there, he'd always had that hunger. Always wanted to be her hero.

However badly what he had said had hurt her, he hadn't meant that hurt. He would never mean that hurt. He was screwed up, just like she was, and he made a lot of mistakes, but he never, ever made them on purpose, never *wanted* to punish her for being. He had so much love in him that he didn't know what to do with it all, and so he had given it to her.

As if he felt her gaze across the distance, Luc lifted his head suddenly and looked across the square and down the street straight at her.

She gave him a shy little wave. *Can we make up now?*

I'm sorry it took me a while, but—you don't understand. You don't understand what it felt like, deep in my womb, when you said something might go wrong.

148

We just need some moments of peace and quiet together, so that we can understand each other. But I need you to want those moments, too.

Luc lifted a hand. But he forgot to wave with it. Instead, it stretched toward her palm up, fingertips curling. *Come back to me.*

"Luc must be deliriously happy," Jaime said, smiling.

Cade grinned. "I have a bet with Sylvain about what he'll have me hunting for at the American store next. Sylvain is having a field day with all this."

"When Sylvain's wife can't even stand the smell of chocolate, we're going to remember how hard he laughed at his fellow chefs," Jaime warned.

Cade slid a wary glance back at the baby store but didn't challenge the assumption that Sylvain might one day have to deal with his wife's morning sickness. "And Dom?"

"I think Dom might need a few more years before he trusts himself to be a father," Jaime said, with a subtle tenderness and patience. "He'll be wonderful at it one day."

Hunh. So even strong people could be nervous about parenthood. It wasn't just something weak or spoiled about her. "Luc," she said firmly, "is going to be wonderful at it, too."

***

"What the hell is this about chocolate?" Sylvain demanded. "Right here it says that chocolate is one of the top ten foods women crave when they're pregnant. It's number two!"

"After ice," Luc said. "And just before lemon. Summer seems to prefer lime."

"'Chocolate,'" Sylvain read. "'Why Pregnant Women Can't Get Enough of It.' *Not* why they flee to a beach house to avoid even smelling it." He turned his head and frowned at his wife, who was exploring Sainte-Mère with Summer and Jaime. The three women were still visible through one of the arches that led away from the *place*. "And ice doesn't even count as a food. So clearly chocolate should be number one."

"How about ginger?" Dom showed the screen of his phone. *Astuces qu'on s'échange entre copines*, it said. Girlfriend tips. "They recommend ginger."

Sylvain leaned forward. "Also Coke." He shook his head. "That's just sick. You can't feed your own child Coke in the womb, Luc. The peanut butter is bad enough."

Luc decided not to confess that before he met Summer, he used to drink Coke at home at one in the morning, to accompany the chips and all the other junk food he was consuming in his greed for effortless calories. All top restaurant chefs did that, as far as he knew, but outside of the Christmas and Easter and Valentine's seasons, chocolate shops had a calmer pacing. Apparently Sylvain managed to remain above all the junk food cravings, and the last thing he wanted to do was confirm any of Sylvain's convictions of superiority.

Summer had taken over feeding him once she found out about the chips and soft drinks. He'd had three months of bliss, leaving the restaurant and arriving home to be *fed*, to be *nourished*, before the baby had stolen it from him by making her too sick to cook. But he forgave the baby. He'd forgive his baby anything.

God. Would his baby forgive him? He didn't want to get anything wrong with his baby, no matter what Sylvain said. He wanted to be perfect for her.

"Luc!" A big voice boomed into his concentration. "Luc Leroi! *Merde, alors!*"

The identity behind the voice penetrated before Luc even finished turning around, easing muscles in him, as if the voice itself was an exuberant embrace. "Gabriel?"

Big, brown-haired, blue-eyed Gabriel Delange was the pastry chef who had once trained Luc himself and who now had a fountain built to him in this very town, and he was larger than life in every way there was. He dropped his wife's hand to reach for Luc's and then, as soon as Luc put his in it, just yanked him forward into a giant hug. "*Petit salaud*, it's about time you came to see me! What are you doing? How's this new restaurant going?"

Smashed up against his chest, Luc tried to process a strong, male hug. Good God, that was two in one week. The last time a man had hugged him before that had been his father's, twenty-one years ago, just before Luc was dragged away from him to a foster home. Even Patrick didn't hug him except in pretense. There was some kind of prickle, of mutual challenge, in their relationship that didn't allow for it.

It felt so disconcertingly as if having arms as strong as his, a body as strong as his, just embrace him with warmth and affection had reached deep inside him and given him something he needed.

Gabriel grabbed his shoulders and pushed him back to look into his face. "Trying to compete with your old chef, are you? We'll see about that."

Luc started to smile. "Worried?"

Gabriel snorted. "No, kid. I taught you everything you know."

Luc's smile grew. "I might have taught myself a few things since then."

"Pfff." Gabriel waved a grandiosely dismissive hand. "I'm not worried about *that*."

Luc laughed, a sound that rang all through him, as if something important had been released. He was not good at laughing. Summer occasionally could get him to laugh from pure happiness, and Patrick with his wicked, twitting humor, prying laughs out of him mercilessly. But even after twelve years of Patrick and six months of Summer, it still wasn't something he did every day. He'd once thought that if Gabriel hadn't gotten fired when Luc was his nineteen-year-old sous-chef, if he'd had a few more years training in the glow of that man's expansive heart, he might have turned out halfway sane.

"Damn, it's good to see you." Gabriel pulled him back in for another spontaneous hug. "I heard you grew up to be all famous and everything." He grinned, since he was at least as famous himself. "Had good training, did you, kid?"

The last time he had seen Gabriel had been a year ago, when Gabe had asked to use Luc's kitchen at the Leucé when he wanted to propose to his girlfriend, Jolie. That man never shrank, did he? All that size, all that heart, all out there. If anything, he was even bigger these days, with a happiness and energy that expanded to fill everything and everyone around him. Luc found himself allowing something close to a grin back. "Well, I might have had a chef once who taught me a thing or two."

"A thing or *two*? Ha! Ungrateful brat. And what are you doing here?" Gabriel turned to Dom. Dom had worked alongside Luc as sous under Gabriel just before Pierre Manon, Jolie's jealous and difficult top chef father, fired Gabe.

Braced, Dom extended his hand, and since Gabriel couldn't yank him off his feet when the man was forewarned, Gabe just surged forward instead and still wrapped Dom up in another big hug, as if rough, big, I-am-the-baddest-man-in-the-room Dom was his personal, cute teddy-bear.

Dom came out of it blinking, entirely befuddled, and...hell, was that a hint of a flush rising on Dom's cheeks? Luc cherished a private glee.

"Sylvain, too? What's the matter?" Gabe demanded of Luc. "Did you have to call on all your Paris friends for help to have a chance at competing with me?" He grinned and then shoved Luc lightly in the shoulder as if he just couldn't contain his energy or happiness. "*Shit*, kid, I can't believe you waited so long before coming to see me. You know, I could have helped you get set up."

It was why Luc hadn't gone to see him when he first opened the restaurant. He didn't know how to be the person who needed help.

"He sulked," Gabriel's wife Jolie informed them, standing up on tiptoe to reach the men's cheeks. Belatedly, Luc bent to exchange kisses with the much smaller, golden-haired woman he'd last seen when Gabe proposed to her in Luc's kitchens. "He brooded and acted all temperamental and swore he was *not* going to go see you first and he stomped around every week and complained you *still* hadn't come see him and...I was seriously about to come hit you over the head to make you behave right."

Luc's eyebrows went up. Jolie thought she could hit him over the head to change his behavior?

How the hell had he gotten so approachable? Being hit over the head by a woman was almost like some weird, affection-starved man's idea of a hug. Like when Summer pretended to smack him on the arm, although she always turned it into a caress instead. He glanced toward Summer, who was looking their way curiously. She and the Corey sisters headed back toward them.

Gabriel had folded his arms and was scowling just at the memory of Luc's behavior, but then he remembered he hadn't properly greeted Sylvain yet and turned to give the chocolatier's hand a firm, friendly shake. "You should have told me you all were in town, we would have had you over for dinner."

By his side, Jolie gave a resigned sigh at the idea of having three of the most famous chocolatiers-pâtissiers in the world over for dinner, but presumably by now she was getting used to it. Hell, her father was Pierre Manon, and she'd been living with Gabriel for a year now. They'd gotten married last winter, just before Luc met Summer. She had to be used to quite a lot, when it came to dealing with top chefs.

"Summer's iffy with dinners right now." Luc waggled a hand in the air to indicate his guess at what was happening inside her tummy. "But why don't you join us tonight at our house?" At least that way, whatever cravings she got, he could leap to satisfy them.

Jolie's head tilted alertly. "She's...iffy...?"

Luc stuffed his hands in his pockets and nodded, feeling so funny. As if this great huge beam was trying to break through his self-control and bask out there in the open air.

"Really?" Jolie broke into a huge grin.

"She's what?" Gabriel looked back and forth between his wife and Luc. "Sick?"

Jolie stood on tiptoe and whispered in Gabriel's ear.

"You're going to have a *baby?*" Gabriel roared so loudly that Summer, coming across the *place* with Cade and Jaime, stopped, clasping her hands to her cheeks. "*Merde!*" Gabe yanked Luc in for another hug and pounded him on his back. "A little Luc? Hell!"

"I keep trying to imagine what repressed, control-freak perfectionism looks like on a three-year-old, but my imagination always fails me," Sylvain said helpfully.

Luc slanted him a dry glance.

"Something like that." Sylvain gestured to Luc's expression. "Only...chubbier cheeks." He approximated a child's round face in the air with those ever-expressive hands of his, puffing air into his own.

"Don't worry," a warm, sandy voice said from behind Luc. "I was planning on making sure the kid had a good role model. You know, someone who could teach him how to leave his clothes scattered all over the floor."

Luc went still. And then he spun to see Patrick lounging against one of the pine trees that shaded the *boules* court. His long, lean form slouched, gold hair tousled, jaw unshaved. "Or her," Patrick said easily. "Or, here's an idea, *twins*. That way, one of each."

"Twins?" An image of two babies depending on him instead of one exploded in Luc's head, and his ears started ringing again.

Patrick grinned and straightened lazily away from the tree to hold out a hand. "Hello, Luc. Heard you were having a hard time living without me."

Luc had never felt so glad to shake a hand in his whole life. He held on too long, as if Patrick was pulling him from a freezing ocean onto his surfboard. "You got here fast."

"You sounded desperate," Patrick said kindly, his mouth laughing while his eyes forgot to, the blue searching and keen. "Of course, I always knew it was just a matter of time before you cracked without me," he added soulfully.

Yes. Luc tried to figure out what to say. In one of the last fights they'd had, they'd each accused the other of being over-dependent. Fights were normal, for two men who had worked twelve years together in brutal, perfectionist conditions. But this one had been pivotal. Soon afterward, they had each chosen different paths, for the first time in twelve years.

"Sylvain. Dom." Patrick shook hands with the other men. "Hell, *Gabe.*" Once a fifteen-year-old apprentice under rising star pastry chef Gabriel Delange, back when Luc was his sous-chef, Patrick now seized the older man's hand in both of his, a huge, delighted grin breaking out on his face. "Gabriel Delange, *hell.*"

Gabriel grinned, and, for good measure, yanked Patrick into a big bear hug, too. Patrick reciprocated with complete aplomb and emerged to kiss Jolie's cheeks and turn back to grin at Luc. "What did you do, call an army?"

"Summer was lonely," Luc protested.

"Ah." Another blue glance from Patrick, his eyes full of wicked laughter. He flexed his shoulders and gazed out at the Alps. "Well, it's a good thing we're up here giving Summer company then, isn't it?" he asked the mountains.

Damn, it felt good to be controlling the urge to strangle Patrick for his ability to skewer straight through to the truth. "She's got her cousins with her!" That was the whole point of this visit.

Seriously. It was.

"Oh, well, that's all right, then," Patrick said. "Sarah is just going to love all that female bonding with a horde of billionaires."

Sarah Lin had been their intern at the Leucé. The fact that Patrick had gotten involved with her despite his role as her supervisor had been a factor in some of Luc's and his fights there at the end. Of course, Luc's tumultuous relationship with Summer Corey, the owner of their hotel, had been another factor.

"You brought Sarah?"

Patrick shrugged. "Can't live without her, really," he said idly, as if it was a joke. Which meant it was profoundly true.

Just then, the women reached them, Sarah slipping up beside Patrick, whose arm immediately looped her into his side, Summer and Cade and Jaime all greeting Patrick and then Gabriel and Jolie with cheek kisses and curious glances. Patrick ruffled Summer's hair and winked at her. Sarah didn't look jealous or threatened in the slightest.

"So." Patrick rubbed his hands together and clapped them. "I know this great place to get drinks around here." He pointed at Luc. "Or it will be a great place after I get done stocking it up." He turned, clearly expecting that one movement to be enough to get everyone to follow him. But he paused just a second gazing at the mountains. "Damn, it's beautiful here. And you never invited me to join you? That hurts my feelings."

Chapter 20

"Diaper changing!" Cade exclaimed. "Bingo. I knew YouTube wouldn't let us down."

The women sat by the infinity pool, its edge seeming to flow right over into the starry yachts floating in the Mediterranean below. It wasn't the Southern Cross, but with friendly female voices floating around Summer—it was a pretty nice view. Because after all, it wasn't the stars that made the Southern Cross so beautiful. It was the people.

"Cade, while you and Sarah are over there making five-year plans, Jolie and I are going to figure out how to get Summer through the first trimester. Have you tried eating crackers before you get out of bed?" Jaime asked Summer. "That's one of the tips here. Pretzels, for example."

"These ice pops are pretty good." Cade waved one of the ones Summer had shared. "Luc's onto something here."

Summer sucked on her own lime ice pop, riding one of those evening waves of nausea again. Leaning back in one of the great canvas chairs, she put her feet up while the other women clicked through web pages. Which made her feel like a fool, of course, the incapable, weak one surrounded by capable women, but every time she tried to lean over to look at the computer screens with them, nausea started winning the battle.

"I don't know if we can trust these lists, though," Cade said. "This one says chocolate is a top craving, and remember what it did to Mom?"

Chocolate. Ugh. Summer tightened her hold on her tummy.

"Exactly," Cade said. "But we'd better not tell Sylvain."

"What about ginger?" Jaime asked. "Ginger ale? I'm sure Luc could make you some with real ginger."

"If you ask Luc Leroi to make ginger ale, he'll do a reverse spherification of it or something like that," Sarah Lin said with a quiet thread of amusement. As one of Luc's former interns, she knew a lot more about what Luc was capable of than even Summer herself did, although Summer was learning as fast as she could.

Summer smiled at Sarah. It was good not to have to be wary of the other woman. Maybe it was the discussions over the phone as Summer tracked down engineering students who could help her, or maybe it was some security Sarah had about Patrick, but Sarah didn't seem to hold that time Patrick had kissed Summer against Summer at all. As if it was just...in the past or something. No threat to her present.

If Summer's tummy wasn't feeling so queasy, she might have hugged her knees with how happy that made her. Just to have...almost *friends.*

"How do you think you do it?" she asked out loud suddenly. "Get a baby right? Not mess it up?" *Not make it turn out lonely and vulnerable, like me. Make sure she knows how to have friends.*

The Corey sisters stopped talking, caught by that question. "You just love it, I guess?" Jaime suggested tentatively.

"Really?" Summer asked, startled with hope. "That's all it takes?" *I can do that!*

Although her parents had always insisted they loved her. This beautiful, delicious forbidden dessert of love that was *supposed* to be hers, if she behaved well enough, and yet somehow, she could never quite taste it.

"I'm pretty sure they have books that expand on the details." Cade tapped into her computer. "Look! *How to Talk So Your Kid Will Listen.* Too bad Dad didn't find that one when you were a kid," she told her sister dryly. "Oh, and here's a whole series about *What to Expect* at every single month of their lives." She opened the sample of one of the books and raised her eyebrows. "Wow. Week by week even. Well, that's helpful. This is great stuff."

"Why do you want to get it right?" Sarah Lin asked suddenly.

"I, well—because it's my baby?" Summer said.

Sarah reached into a little leather backpack purse at the wall by her feet and pulled out a small leather notebook, its cover embossed with a silver heart signed with the initial P. "Could I show you something?"

She opened it and held it out to Summer. The other women leaned in, and they all looked in some puzzlement at notes about sugar sculpting, written so carefully the letters looked like print.

"My mother wanted to get my sister and me right." Sarah traced the letters with her finger. "That's why I write like this. She didn't know. She was illiterate herself back then, training herself at the same time as us. But she looked at books and thought if we could write exactly like the letters in books, we would be writing perfectly. She wanted the world to love us." Sarah flipped a few pages to a sprawling signature, the only legible part of which was a big P that matched the silver-embossed P on the journal's cover and there, possibly, a capital C. "That's how Patrick writes. And really, of the two of us, who do you find easier to love?"

Patrick. He swept everyone into his charm, while Sarah Lin kept in this contained, quiet space of hers, into which no one could step very easily.

"I'm not trying to criticize my mother," Sarah said. "She loves us with everything in her, and she would do anything for us. But I don't know. Kids aren't bonsai. Maybe instead of trying to make them beautiful to the rest of the world, you should just love them and let them grow."

Summer was positive she could love her child and let the child grow. But...grow how?

"But you have to teach them a work ethic," Cade pointed out.

"And to look out for those less fortunate than they are," Jaime said.

"And a certain degree of manners is probably a good idea, to get along with the world," Summer added uneasily. Although deep down what she really wanted to teach her daughter was how to tell the world *Fuck you.* And mean it. Really not care. That thing Cade and Jaime's dad and her own did, that let both Mack and Sam Corey stomp right after what they wanted and not give a crap who hated them for it. "Oh, God." She pressed her hand into her belly. "This is so complicated."

"We all turned out all right," Cade pointed out, gesturing to include everyone in the group. "Although our parents didn't get everything perfect. Trust me, that time Jaime stowed away in my car to sneak into a rock concert she was too young for and I was the one who lost driving privileges was completely unfair. Plus, I mentioned about the heels, right?"

Plus, Cade and Jaime's mother had died when they were still young, a brutal abandonment beyond her control but also beyond appeal. Julie Corey's death had made Summer feel as if she'd lost her last hope, so she couldn't even imagine how hard it had hit Julie's own daughters.

"Speak for yourselves," Summer muttered, sinking more deeply into her chair. Her nausea stirred, not liking the way her slump folded her belly. She did not feel "all right" at all.

"You turned out just fine, too, Summer," Jaime said wryly. "We all feel that way sometimes."

"You do?" Really? They were so confident.

"People don't tend to go on crusades to save the world because they feel just fine with who they are sitting on the couch watching TV," Sarah pointed out.

Oh. "But you're amazing," Summer told crusader Jaime incredulously.

"You know, you're a pretty cool person yourself," Jaime said gently. "A lot of kids certainly think so, which is a pretty positive sign, don't you think, about how well you'll do with your own?"

Summer gazed out over the sea, trying to digest that. The praise wanted to dissolve through her, wanted to nurture her belief in herself, but there was this dark, bitter doubt that came out to attack it, nastily. "Anyway, I've got back-up," she said wryly, letting it leak out.

"Exactly," Jaime said. "I mean, if you think Cade would let you get away with doing something she thought was wrong without telling you, boy, do you not know her. I'll be more discreet, of course."

Summer stared at the sisters. Warmth flooded her, out of nowhere, so much warmth she didn't even know what to do with it. It wanted to come out as tears. "I meant—I meant, ah—" She swallowed. "My mother is interviewing nannies for me. It wasn't my idea," she added hastily, as all the other women looked taken aback. "She thought I would need one. She promised to find one good enough that I couldn't screw up the baby." *Because that worked out so well with me. Here I am, not screwed up at all.*

And she'd had a really good nanny, too. Liz. Kind of her lifeline back then.

All the other women were staring at her. She tried to shrug.

"When people shape you when you're tiny, it can be really hard to break out of that mold, can't it?" Sarah said very softly, almost to herself.

"Summer, allow me to share with you one of my favorite phrases. My dad taught it to me, for when I have to go into a boardroom and make a decision that I know everyone is going to criticize, everyone is going to call me a bitch for," Cade said. "You might want to practice it for situations like this. It goes: *Screw you.*"

"That's not what Dad actually says," Jaime mentioned, amused.

"Well...his version starts with an F," Cade admitted. "He felt that *screw* might not be powerful enough for all occasions. So you can use that, too."

"Yeah, but...you can't say that to your own mother, Cade," Jaime protested.

"In your head." Cade tapped her skull. "It's the general idea. You think it, when all the worries get to you, and then you roll over and tuck yourself up against Syl—Luc and go to sleep."

"It does kind of work like that sometimes," Jaime admitted. "Having that person to tuck yourself into definitely helps handle anything."

Sarah nodded.

Summer lay back in her chair and sucked on the last little bit of her ice pop. "I wonder if it works the other way?"

The women looked inquiring.

"That guys need to roll over and tuck themselves up into the other person sometimes, too. To handle things."

Everyone considered that. "They don't tuck very well," Jaime decided finally. Summer bit back a grin at the image of rough, muscled Dom tucking his head in Jaime's lap.

Although...that was oddly easy to imagine.

"I think we're more like their teddy-bear sometimes," Jolie said. "You know—we get pulled in and held tight. And *that's* what reassures them."

Now all the women were blushing a little, looking out to sea, growing thoughtful and quiet.

Maybe Summer and Luc needed to find more time to do these things. Maybe...maybe Summer needed to be the one who made sure they did.

Something eased suddenly, with all these women around her. Luc had always had trouble finding the right way to show his feelings, outside his desserts. He had always panicked. He had always pushed too hard and held on too tight, then let go at the wrong moment because he started fearing his own tight, greedy hold.

But he did love her. Which gave her all the power anyone could ever need. The power to say, *Luc. Let's talk.*

"You know what I think?" Jolie asked suddenly. "I think the most important thing you can do for your baby is give it a happy family. Parents who stick together and spend time with her. That kind of thing."

Everyone looked at her, and she shrugged a little, visibly uneasy at the attention and probably what she had just revealed about her own childhood. "That's just my two cents."

***

"This is ridiculous," Sylvain said. "This one says chocolate is a top craving, too." He slumped broodingly on the floor, his back against the couch. "The Corey women were warped from birth," he muttered. "That's the only explanation."

Slouching himself as usual, Patrick took a healthy swallow of his wine and grinned like a man who had no paternal cares in the world. Easy enough for him, Luc thought. It would be far too premature for Patrick and Sarah to be thinking kids already. Patrick had a lot on his plate as he made a new future for himself. And he and Sarah had barely known each other for…

For six months longer than Luc and Summer had. Luc frowned at his wine glass, a little confused by it. It stood resolutely half-full, the way he liked it, and yet he felt so much more relaxed and easy than he had before they had all ended up on the floor with the wine bottle and their computers out. Relaxed, as if the blunt realization that he and Summer had been a *little* fast about jumping into the baby thing wasn't a question for angst and crises but just a rather funny bit of precipitousness on their part that they now had to deal with.

It might make things a little complicated, a little challenging. But no end of the world, or their relationship, or happiness as he knew it, loomed in sight.

In fact, he felt so much more comfortable at the idea of dealing with it—happy, relaxed—that he kept suspecting alcohol was involved.

But Dom sat on the other side of his wine glass, and Dom never touched alcohol at all much less fed it to unwitting others. And even Patrick couldn't manage to surreptitiously re-half-fill Luc's glass regularly from his slouching position on the other side of Sylvain.

Besides, Patrick and Sylvain and Gabriel seemed to be enjoying sharing the bottle themselves.

"You'd think candied ginger dipped in chocolate would be perfect for any sane pregnant woman," Sylvain said broodingly. "One that wasn't genetically scarred." He gave his wedding ring a darkling glance, presumably in lieu of his wife.

"This one says carbonated beverages. I could make a ginger syrup, mix it with spring water, and carbonate it." Luc rubbed his thumb against the rug under him, tasting variations without ever parting his lips. His taste receptors actually activated for the combinations he imagined, so well-trained by now. But did they activate the same way Summer's did, now that pregnancy had turned her taste buds so crazy? "Maybe with a squeeze of fresh lime."

"You could do a frozen reverse spherification of it," Gabriel said. "The calcium lactate's probably good for pregnant women, right? Don't they need extra calcium? You want me to whip something up right now and see if she likes it?"

No, Luc did not want him to do that, *merde*. All these greedy men around him trying to feed his wife and baby instead of him. *Back off. She's mine to feed.*

"How'd she like the peaches?" asked Nico, who had somehow ended up in the gathering, too. Luc wasn't even entirely sure how that had happened. They were colleagues, weren't they? Surely they weren't friends already? Despite how much Nico seemed to be amused by him. The other person who was frequently amused by Luc, Patrick, kept eyeing the other chef in this lazy, alert way as if he hadn't decided what he thought about him yet.

"Maybe it's that Corey *merde* their mother was tortured with. That's got to be it," Sylvain said. "Probably she would have loved *good* chocolate."

"'Feed her before she gets out of bed'," Dom read, ignoring Sylvain. "Have you tried that?"

"Have you tried asking her what she wants?" Patrick asked, with the air of a man suggesting a radical new medical approach to curing cancer. Luc slanted him a glance.

Patrick widened his eyes. "What? I hear there are men who talk to their wives about what they want. It's not a widespread practice or anything yet, don't worry, but it might have potential."

God, he had missed the regular urge to throw something at Patrick's head. All those years in the kitchen, and he'd restrained himself every time. So many interesting foods around to dump on a guy's head, too.

"*Pickles,*" Luc said carefully in English, since the damn things she liked had no resemblance at all to any *cornichons* he knew of. He couldn't say a single full sentence in English—except *I love you,* which he'd been fortunate enough to be exposed to a lot recently—but he'd picked up a fair amount of food vocabulary in the past fifteen years in top kitchens. "That's what she said she wanted. And *peanut butter. Peaches. Popsicles.*"

"Wow." Patrick put a hand over his heart. "That accent. Say something else?" He fanned himself.

Luc sighed heavily.

Patrick grinned.

The corners of Luc's lips kicked up, and all that anxiety that had weighed on his heart felt so damn *light*.

"So we've discovered she likes alliteration," Patrick said with great thoughtfulness. "What other things start with P in English?" He made an elaborate show of searching on his phone. "Oh, look, peas. And pretzels. There you go, Luc. Have you tried that?"

"Pretzels is on this list," Dom said, from his laptop. He turned it toward them. "Really."

"It's practically poetry," Patrick said, awed. "How about potatoes?"

Luc almost laughed.

Patrick's grin deepened. "If Sylvain and Gabe and I get any drunker, you won't have an inhibition left. Ignore Dom brooding over there in the corner. We'll drug his water." He put up a hand for an exaggerated stage-whisper to Dom. "*It's in the ice cubes.*"

Dom flicked a melting fragment of ice at him.

"*Ice!*" Patrick exclaimed, sucking the fragment into his mouth. "That's on the lists! You're a genius! And here I thought you were nothing more than brute muscle."

Dom sighed so heavily that it made Luc's sigh seem a shallow breath. Luc discovered a grin on his face and couldn't even figure out how it had gotten there.

He looked up at movement in the doorway. Summer, in yoga pants and a silky top, ready for bed except for the bra she had kept on in honor of their guests. "Are you guys still up?" Her gaze rested on Luc.

He grinned at her from the floor, feeling so relaxed he was almost foolish with it. *Hey, we're all right, did you know that? Our worries are silly, not serious.*

Summer's expression softened, bemused. She tilted her head, blue gaze tracing over him, curious and warm.

He blew her a tiny kiss.

"Are you drunk?" she asked curiously.

"Oh, you know, five sips," Patrick said. "About the same amount he had that night he met you."

166

"You only had five sips the night you met me?" Summer asked. "You always told me you'd been drinking champagne!"

"Hmm. Such a strange sensitivity to alcohol, don't you think?" Patrick rolled his eyes to heaven. "Almost as if that's nothing to do with what's going on at all."

Summer took a step into the room and then hesitated and stepped back to the door. "I won't interrupt your—your guy thing."

Luc patted the floor beside him.

"Hell, no," Patrick said. "If you get to have Summer in here, I get to have Sarah. No fair."

"You're the one who told me to ask her what she wants," Luc pointed out to him.

Patrick took another swallow of his wine. "That conversation was intended for your more private moments," he said loftily.

A black head appeared behind Summer and then slipped past her in the doorway. Patrick grinned in delight and lifted an arm so that Sarah could more comfortably tuck herself up within it when she sat beside him. How they had all ended up on the floor when they had perfectly good furniture, Luc wasn't entirely sure.

The other women followed, laughing, Cade and Jaime and Jolie maybe just the tiniest bit over-relaxed from liquor. Dom pulled Jaime down to sit between his knees with her back against his chest, and Cade took the corner of the couch behind Sylvain, folding her legs up and rubbing his head when he rested it back against her calves.

Nico shifted, this slightest angling of his body away from all that couple-happiness in the room. His relaxed demeanor closed just a little, but that was the only sign he gave that he was the odd man out—the one person there who didn't have someone to curl up with him.

Well, and Luc.

Luc patted the floor again, his heart starting to tighten as it braced for rejection. His wife was the only one still standing in the doorway.

"We've got beds for everyone if anyone is getting tired," Summer said. "That's what I came to tell you."

"The night's young," Luc said with a wave of his hand. Well, for chefs it was young. Barely midnight.

Sylvain smiled in this slight way, amusement packed with understanding. "We're staying tomorrow, too, you know." *You don't have to get all the friendship and support you can out of us tonight.*

"Sarah and I were just planning to move in," Patrick said. "I mean, I only have this big a glimpse of Notre-Dame from my apartment." He held up thumb and forefinger. "And you guys have the whole Mediterranean. Plus, I hear you're going to need an *au pair* soon to help take care of that baby."

The tiniest stiffening on Summer's part. Luc's focus on her sharpened.

"*And* I freeze fantastic ice cubes," Patrick said, and Luc knew he'd caught that stiffening, too, and was easing it away. "Which I hear is all you're eating these days. *Way* better ice cubes than this guy. His are all—dense. He uses inferior water."

Summer laughed, a surprised, delighted sound, and Luc relaxed again. Damn, it was good to have Patrick around. He didn't even feel jealous of the laughter, just...happy. Happy that Summer was genuinely smiling.

Patrick folded an arm behind his head. "Now if *Sarah* were pregnant, I'd have to make all her ice cubes in the form of...hearts." He turned his head to gaze down at his girlfriend a moment, his smile sinking inward, to secrets, as his hand rubbed her shoulder. "Yeah. But you *know* how bad Luc is at putting his heart out there through food."

Summer actually giggled, her hand covering her mouth, her eyes sparkling at Luc. All the love in those eyes, all softened and freed by humor.

Oh.

Oh...we're going to be all right.

Thank you, Patrick. For getting my head back on straight.

"I suppose you'd make the pickles heart-shaped, too?" Luc asked dryly, but he couldn't pull his gaze away from Summer.

"No, I never mess with a good phallic shape," Patrick said, with an airy and outrageous wave of his hand. He sent Summer a limpidly innocent look. "Do you?" He lifted Sarah's hand to his lips and kissed it, automatically reassuring her that his teasing of another woman had no serious undertones.

Summer gave another little gulp of a giggle and then just burst out laughing, her eyes dancing even as she tried to make them wide and innocent, shaking her head as if she had no idea even what a phallic shape was.

"I'm going to have to hit you again," Luc mentioned to Patrick.

"And I don't even work for you anymore this time." Patrick sighed despairingly. "What a waste of a chance for a lawsuit."

Summer slipped into the room and curled up against Luc, laughing more and more as Patrick expanded into the laughter with great enjoyment, growing more and more outrageous with each success. Luc covered her hand, resting on his abdomen, and played with it gently while her laughter grew first more relaxed, then softer and softer. It must have been an hour later when he looked down and discovered she was fast asleep.

Patrick slouched back against the base of the chair, with Sarah asleep against his own shoulder, and toasted his wine glass to—apparently himself. Patrick drank a long swallow of his wine with an expression of smug satisfaction. "You're an idiot," he told Luc. "Have I mentioned it to you lately?"

Damn but he'd missed Patrick. "You're not supposed to call your chef an idiot, you know."

Patrick shook his head, but didn't correct the title of chef to their current relationship. "Go take your wife to bed, idiot."

Chapter 21

G od, that felt good, the weight of his wife against his arms and chest, the thought of that little baby, right there in her belly, still so tiny it didn't add anything to her weight at all. It felt as if he could take care of them. It felt as if they were all his.

It felt strong, and it felt awkward, too, this new, fresh caution about all the things that he might do or be wrong. Was the scent of him, or the motion, stirring up nausea? Odd and disturbing, how much the changes inside her could change their relationship, when he hadn't changed at all—the scent of her still made him feel as if he had come home.

Until he found her, or she found him, the kitchen had been the only home he had, his apartment no more than a place to eat potato chips, watch TV until the adrenaline released him, and sleep.

Now he had her, for his home. But...

"It's my security," he whispered to her. "The restaurant. When I'm worried, it's where I know I can get everything right."

"Mmm?" A sleepy, questioning noise from Summer as he lowered her onto the mattress. He folded the comforter over her and knelt by the side of the bed. Maybe he knelt because he still didn't feel he had the right to get back in that bed with her, or maybe it was because it put his face so much nearer her belly. She patted sleepily with her hand, her eyes still closed, trying to pat him, ending up patting his head. "'Sokay," she mumbled. "I know."

Of course she forgave him.

Of course she did.

She loves me.

He curved his hand over her belly. It was warm and flat, just her ordinary belly, and yet life beat out of it suddenly into his palm like a pulsing sun. *God, mine? Mine. Some of me, right there. Growing.*

"Thanks for inviting everyone," she murmured and snuggled her head into the pillow. He sat on the edge of the bed, watching his hand on her belly, watching her face as she fell completely back asleep.

After a long time, he went to their closet. The walk-in was much bigger than any closet he'd ever had outside restaurant pantries, and in it, he could move down this short, lovely alley between his clothes and Summer's. His fingers brushed over her dresses, releasing soft hints of her scent into the air, soft memories of her body being touched by him through those clothes.

He'd changed lodgings several times since he first started collecting treasures, but he always tucked this box into the same place: the deepest corner of the closet, the last thing in the house anyone might find, if they wanted to steal it.

A small, worn cardboard box that he had pulled out of the trash just after he was first fostered, its flaps all bent from being opened and tucked into each other again and again, its corners battered. In clumsy marker, it said "Luc". Then, a little older and neater above it, "Luc Leroi." "Mine," he had written in another spot, bolding it, shaping the letters into a stamp. Around the words were drawn layers of things: monsters and sharks and superheroes in different colored markers and with different levels of skill, whatever he believed in, at that particular age, whatever he placed his hopes in, to protect that box.

He opened it slowly. Every time he opened that old carton his heart tightened with panic, until that sudden, blissful release when he saw that his little collection was all still there. A teddy-bear a child had forgotten in a park and he had kept for his, an old Hot Wheels car he'd found under a Métro seat. A shell he'd found and used at school once to pretend he'd been to the beach.

And...a little girl's bracelet. He drew it out as carefully as if the jewels and gold could shatter like sugar. He used to assume the gold was fake, the jewels that formed the flowers only crystal. Now he knew better. He knew that his father could have sold it for enough to feed them for weeks, maybe months.

Luc had gone hungry often back then. But he was glad he had never shown it to his father, glad neither of them had realized that he could have traded this for a hundred of those éclairs that he had always dreamed about in the shop windows.

"Luc?" Summer asked very softly, from the closet door.

He tried to smile at her, but he couldn't quite. His heart was too full.

She twisted the knob for the closet lighting just enough to provide a gentle dimness and came to kneel in front of him. "Hey," she said, and touched his cheek. "Are you all right?"

"Yes." But his eyes stung, and his throat felt too tight.

So she didn't believe him, because she *loved* him, she cared about him, and her hand stroked his cheek as her gaze went over what was in his lap and in his hand. He'd never shown the box to her, his meager treasures too vulnerable to share with his heiress wife. "What's this?" She touched his wrist very gently but didn't quite touch the bracelet in it. As if she knew it might be too precious for him to share even with her.

"You don't recognize it?"

She shook her head, puzzled. But she touched it now, just delicately, then lifted it a little in her fingers, studying it.

Of course she wouldn't. She would have been five or six, as he had been nine or ten. The bracelet would have been replaced, would have blurred with all the other jewels she would have had. "You gave it one day to a boy you met in a park. A dark-haired boy. Remember?"

Her eyes widened. "I gave this to you?"

"We talked about it once." Maybe they had never talked about it more because it was too delicate a fancy. What if on closer inspection, it turned out they were wrong? That he hadn't been the dark-haired little boy she remembered from that park, and his little golden princess was some other little girl.

Her fingers tightened on it. "I guess I didn't—" She broke off.

Yeah. *Didn't want to question it too closely. Didn't want to risk believing in it enough to put it to the test.*

"I got in trouble," she remembered suddenly. "For being careless with my things. For being...spoiled." Her smile twisted. "I think I was sent to my room alone and denied dessert."

Her goddamn parents. "It made all the difference to me," he said fiercely. "Back then. You don't know how hard I held onto it, when I needed to dream of being something better. Of having something beautiful."

Her eyes shimmered. "Luc." She touched his face. "*You* are the beauty. You have no idea, do you, how beautiful you are. Not the things you make. You." Her hand cupped his cheek. "So you see...you did, indeed, make a thing of beauty that no one could ever steal from you."

God, she hurt his heart. It was as if that heart couldn't get used to thumping so hard from joy and kept bruising itself on its own happiness. Who knew that even happiness required you to be tough enough to brave it? He lifted her hand, clutched around his bracelet, and kissed it. "You've got all the desserts you want now."

"Oh, Luc." She petted his chest. "All this heart in you. Sometimes I just can't believe it's all for me."

He covered her hand, holding it tight to the beat of his heart. "It is, though."

She was trying not to cry, her face so soft from tenderness and emotion. She brought her head in to rest against the join of his shoulder, and a little sigh escaped against his throat. Barely louder than a breath, she whispered, "I'm still alone sometimes, though."

He wrapped an arm around her and pulled her closer to him, even though it crushed a battered corner of his box. He'd crushed that carton in his arms so many times. It was good to have something that was his that wasn't a thing, and that couldn't fit in a carton. Even if it was terrifying that his very special non-thing had legs and could walk away. "I'm sorry," he said very softly. "I just—I think I'm still a little messed up."

"Yeah." She brought his hand to her mouth and cradled it there, so that he could feel the soft pressure of her lips as she spoke. "Me, too."

"I'm really sorry," he whispered to her. "I want that baby so bad, it's just...I can't stand it. All the ways I can lose you both just keep clawing their way out of this box I try to lock them in and crawling through my brain. I *hate them.*" Those damn crawling monster thoughts. *"And I can't stop them."*

She loosed his hand to place both of hers on his shoulders, stroking downward in soothing, petting motions. As if he was in a nightmare.

Yeah, he had monsters in his head with an IQ of ten. Summer didn't have an atom in her capable of abandoning her child to unhappiness.

"That's why I work so late," he said, low. "I can control that. Whether that restaurant succeeds or not is entirely in my power."

"It's okay, Luc," she whispered. "I told you it was okay."

"I know," he admitted. He just...couldn't make himself believe her. Kept seeing it all shatter in his hands or get eaten by a greedy world.

She eased the bracelet from between their bodies and looked at it, gleaming and pretty and so little-girlish in her hand.

"Why did you give it to him?" Luc asked.

175

"Because he was so nice to me," she said. "He made me feel so special. He was like this superhero. He could do *everything*, climb all the bars, and he took time and lifted me up for them. He played with me. He was special." Her thumb traced over his cheekbones. "Why did you keep it?"

"I wanted to keep her," he said very low. "And I couldn't."

She shifted the box enough that it was on her lap and she could nestle completely into his, wrapping her arms around him hard.

"I've never been able to keep anything," he said through his tight throat, into her hair.

Her arms tightened still harder. "You've got *me*," she said. Then brought his hand to her belly. "Us."

"Your island—"

"A visit, Luc. A *visit*. Because they're my friends, and I miss them, and I want to tell them the news in person and see them be *happy* for me. You knew I'd miss them and want to go back to see them sometimes. We talked about it. You even said once you might try to close the new restaurant for a month every year, in August, and we would spend that month together on Manunui."

"Summer." He could barely say it out loud. "It's all I can do not to cut your passport into shreds. Fifty times a day I have to stop myself. I know what I promised you, about seeing your island. You just—you don't know how bad I am. Inside."

Her eyes had widened, at the threat to her passport. She frowned a little at him and sat up to frame both his cheeks with her hands, the bracelet pressing between her palm and his skin. "Yeah, that's not good. You've got to build a little more trust than that, Luc. I can't be your prisoner."

"I know," he said, defeated. He just didn't know how to do it. Even right now, with her in his lap making it so obvious that she loved him, panic raked claws along his

176

insides at the thought of her going to that island without him.

She gazed at him a long moment, and he tried not to close his eyes in shame. She was trying to make a life with him and all that mess he hid inside his soul. He had to have the guts to let her see what that mess was. To let her know that he was so damn far from that perfect he wished he could be.

"Sometimes," she said softly, "when trust muscles have been atrophied, they take a long, long time to grow. And a lot of work. And it's painful and it hurts, and you have to keep going. You have to yell at yourself to push harder sometimes and not give up. Go through trust physical therapy."

"Is that what you do?" he realized, stroking his hands over her hair. "Force yourself over and over to keep going, whenever you start believing I can't possibly love you?"

Her eyes filled with tears, just like that. It was so easy to touch something vulnerable, with Summer, when you touched close to her heart. She blinked them back, but admitted, low, "There's always this other voice. That says I'm not worth that, so how can you?"

"Do you tell it to shut the hell up?"

"I do," she said firmly.

"Yes." He sighed. "Me, too."

She curled against him, petting his chest, easing with every stroke the fear and tension in him, calming those monster thoughts into quiescence. They slipped away from her touch and scent, like shadows fleeing light. Oh, God, he needed so much more of this—this talking, this stroking. Even if he never won another star in his life, he had to make time for this.

"I'm going to make you a new bracelet," she whispered. "Something you can look at and be reminded that I'll always love you."

"I think that's what my wedding ring is supposed to do," he admitted, stretching the fingers of his left hand.

She stroked it. God, he loved the feel of her fingers there at those hypersensitive, hypertense bases of his. Sometimes it was all he could do not to beg her to keep rubbing his hand forever. "So you need more," she said matter-of-factly. "That's okay."

"You, too, don't you?" He rubbed his fingers over her own wedding ring. "You need more from me."

She was silent for a moment. "I just need you, Luc." She looked up at him. "You to touch me. You to go shopping with me. You to hold my hand and talk to me about the baby. I don't need you to do greater, bigger, more perfect and amazing things. I just need you to be there sometimes when I'm scared and lonely."

It hurt him in this fierce, deep way, to think that he had left her scared and lonely. He hugged her in tight, rubbing her back. "What scares *you*?"

Again the threat of tears shimmered, all those pregnancy hormones finding all her vulnerabilities and playing them up. "Luc. Sometimes *everything* scares me. I try so hard to be like Cade and Jaime, with all their confidence, or like Jolie, just cheerful and happy, or like Sarah, so strong and persistent. And I just—I'm not like *any* of them. I'm *scared* I'll mess up my baby. I'm scared I'll make her turn out like me." And then she did start to cry, breaking Luc's heart.

"Giving?" Luc said, so *furious* with all the world, with her parents. He'd fucking *hit* her father if Sam Corey dared come down for their baby's birth. "Sweet? Smart? Kind to small children?"

Summer shook her head. "That's not enough, Luc. I want her to be *brave*."

"Brave enough to risk her heart over and over? Brave enough to make a new life for herself on a remote island in the South Pacific? Brave enough to make another new life here, for love?"

"Luc," she protested, almost angry. "You know that's not—I mean *really brave*. Tough. Sure of herself."

He tilted her back in his arms to kiss her. "You know the only way I would want our daughter to be different from you, Summer? I want her to believe she's loved. That I love her. That you love her. And that one day, she'll deserve someone else's love, too. And I think we can give her that."

Yes. All at once, he was absolutely certain. And with that certainty, all the rest of the fears fell away. Yes, he could love his daughter or his son: take time with them, play with them, make special things for them, just, damn it, *love them.*

And count on Summer to love them herself, because of course she would, but also—to make sure they knew Luc loved them, too. To guide him, if she thought he wasn't doing something right. "You'll help me, won't you, Summer?" He rubbed that bracelet against her palm.

"Oh, Luc." She threw her arms suddenly around his shoulders and kissed his neck. "You're so much better at loving than you realize."

"I still want your help," he insisted.

She shook her head a little against his throat, but her lips brushed his skin with each shake. "All right."

His heart eased. "You could start right now," he murmured. "You could let me know how I could take care of my baby's mommy."

That word. *Maman.* That he had never, ever been able to say, except as an absence.

That was going to become such a beautiful word.

It hurt how beautiful, but...he thought he could learn to stand it. He thought that hurt might change over time into the most extraordinary joy in the world.

"I just need us to talk more." Summer snuggled into him. "Times like this...that's all I really need. It helps so much."

"Yes," he agreed, this sigh in his voice like a fatigued soldier slumping at last to rest. "It definitely does." For a little while, they were quiet, just absorbing the scent and feel of each other. That utterly beautiful scent and texture of love.

"You know what else I think?" he asked softly, petting her hair. "You'll worry too much, and I'll worry too much, and maybe I'll need you to remind me to step outside my comfort zone and relax. Maybe you'll have to nag me about that. Maybe, even, all my life you might have to nag me about that. It's okay, though, if you nag me, Summer. I'll still love you, even if you have some needs."

She bit her lip and gave the tiniest sniffle and that infuriating smile of hers that meant she was trying to hide the sniffle.

"I *want* to be the person you nag, Summer. I *need* you to. It's good for me. It reminds me there are more parts of me that are important to you than the ones you can eat."

Now the smile that kicked across her face was real and involuntary. "You idiot," she said lovingly. "You always get so stuck on that. As if that's all to you there is."

Yeah. And it made him feel so weird, and giddy, and *good* to know there was more to him. But vulnerable. God, so exposed, in all his messy insides. Desserts were the only part of him he knew he could get absolutely right. Good enough for her.

Thus his rapid descent into paranoia and obsession when he'd lost that security.

Thank God for Patrick, and Sylvain, and Dom, and Nico, and Gabriel. To wiggle their humor and camaraderie into his life, to remind him that there was more to living than being perfect all the time. "Maybe we'll even need some friends to help us relax. But it will be all right. We've made a few friends in our lives, and— we *made* them, you know? We did things that made them like us and want to help us in return. That's why people love you so much on your island. Because you taught every one of their kids with your whole heart, and, knowing you, were as polite and smiling as you could possibly be to every single person you met."

"It's not working so well here," she said wistfully.

"We've only been here three months. Give it time." He didn't quite himself believe it. He'd invested *twelve years* of care and mentoring and fighting and working together, of friendship and more, into Patrick. He might never in his life develop another friend that good.

But...he thought about Nico. Sylvain. Dom. Gabe. There were people around him willing to give a deeper friendship with him a try.

"And I don't see why it would be so bad for me to take a trip for a week back to see all my friends on Manunui. They'd be thrilled."

Oh, yes, they would show her how thrilled they were so much better than he would. She would feel so happy and secure. It would be quite the contrast to his stupid, screwed-up, obsessive, panicked way of loving her.

Of course, if she got tempted to stay there, he could track her down. Take time to relax himself. Enjoy how happy she was there and bring her back with him, refreshed. He'd chased her down to her island once before and found she had already turned around and headed straight back across the world to him, because she missed him so much.

It was *healthy* that she needed her friends in moments like this. It *didn't* mean she was leaving him.

He leaned back against the coats, so that her weight settled more onto him as he petted her. The weight of her head on his heart made that stupid, paranoid organ slowly calm down and beat correctly, with some kind of sane rhythm. His eyes closed, and he concentrated on the textures under his fingers as he drew them over her shoulder, down her arm, all the way down to her slender wrist. He circled it, tracing the bones.

"There's a story," he said. "About a man who let a woman go, when she wanted to go so desperately. And she didn't come back, and she didn't come back...and he died."

"Beauty and the Beast?" she asked doubtfully, pushing herself up onto an elbow to look down at him. Her elbow applied pressure at just the wrong point on his chest, but he didn't tell her it hurt. He liked knowing he could handle any kind of pain as long as she was there.

"That's the one."

"He didn't die. She came back."

"Oh." He'd read all the fairy stories to himself, as research for desserts. Because, as he told Patrick when they were teenagers, and as his own chef Gabriel Delange had once told him, *If we want to make people's dreams, we have to know what those are.* But somehow he always saw that Beast dying of despair. "Not until he'd given up on her and nearly died of loss. Not until after she'd betrayed him."

"Maybe he didn't trust her enough, or himself," Summer said quietly and firmly, holding his eyes. "I mean, in the story, she only went to see her family and stayed a couple of days longer than she originally planned. That's kind of a lot to die over, don't you think? Maybe he was acting kind of nuts."

His mouth twisted. "I'm not sure I'm entirely sane, Summer."

She touched his twisted lips, tracing over them until they softened again. God, that felt so good. He held still for it, soaking up every bit of sensation from her fingertips into him. "You could go with me," she said softly. "You're not actually the Beast or the Lord of Hell, Luc, who can't step free into the sunlit world. But it's true that I assumed you couldn't get away."

He couldn't. But, God, he'd far rather trust his restaurant to the hands of an inexperienced *second* and a chef de cuisine who wanted to turn it into a soup kitchen than trust her to go back to a place she was happy and still return to him.

And, *merde*, but was that ever a sad reflection on his ability to handle a relationship. "I should trust you, I know," he said.

"You should," she agreed. "But I guess you don't know how yet. Trust therapy still in order."

The tense muscles in his face eased at her quiet tone. That was Summer. She denigrated every single negative feeling she had, but she accepted even his most inappropriate, craziest ones as just the way he was. *You're all right. I love you just the way you are.* But she never quite believed he could do the same.

"You're like one of your brand-new interns," she said. "You have to practice at this relationship stuff."

His heart lightened. That was...oddly apt. Envisioning himself as a clumsy intern in love made him want to laugh. He'd *been* a clumsy beginner in pastry once, after all. He'd gotten where he was today, from that clumsy beginning.

She held up her pinched thumb and forefinger. "Maybe next year, or the year after, your trust muscles will have grown bigger." Judging by the three-centimeter gap to which she opened thumb and forefinger, she wasn't expecting any huge trust-on-steroids growth there.

He caught her hand and pulled it back to his lips to kiss it. "You don't mind my baby steps?"

"Luc." She sighed. But patiently. A sigh filled with patience. "You know, I really, really love you."

That made the biggest smile break out on his face. He couldn't help it. He knew it probably looked ridiculous—he wasn't, by nature, someone full of smiles—and yet sometimes she made every cell in his body glow.

"Besides, I kind of like you being clumsy at it. I mean, sometimes it hurts, but it also means it's all new to you, and important enough for you to try with all your heart."

Well...yes. He laid his hand over her heart. That fragile, stubborn heart that had let itself get broken over and over in her search for love, until she found him. "You realize you're kind of an intern at all this, too?"

"Oh, God, yes." She dropped her head to his chest. "We *really* rushed into things, didn't we?"

He petted her head and twined a lock of her hair around his fingers to give her a little tug so she would let him see her face again. "But we'll manage," he told her firmly.

It seemed to be the right thing to say. Her eyes lit, and a real smile blazed out. "Yes," she agreed, equally firmly. And then: "But you have to help me shop for baby things."

"I'll take time off." And pray no critics came. Or maybe think about what Nico had said, about priorities.

"And, Luc—if you can't come to Manunui with me and I go by myself, and after two days of travel to get there I find out someone is getting married the next weekend and they would love it so much if I stayed on a couple of days extra to be part of it—you have to *tough it up*, Luc. Relax. Trust me. You can't die of despair."

"Oh, God." He closed his eyes. Imagining her not showing up when he expected, and not showing up, and... "Will you at least *call?*"

"Sometimes I *can't,* Luc." She sat up astride him. "They need another satellite in that region. And my father is not exactly in any hurry to fulfill that promise to invest in one."

He dragged a hand over his face rather than let her see the truth of him again: *I really don't know if I can handle that.*

Except...the whole point of this conversation was to let her see the truth of him. To let her understand what a mess he was. "I'll go with you."

"I'd like it better if you went with me, anyway," she said softly. "I love it with you on the island. But I'm not trying to threaten you into it."

"I know." He pressed his hand against her belly again. "Summer—" This was an even scarier topic than her island. He almost couldn't broach it. But he had to. "Why are you so worried about miscarriages?" His voice was barely over a whisper. "Is there a reason?"

Her face shuttered. She tried to cover it with one of her careless, absent smiles, but she couldn't, quite. "Just something my mother said. And other people say. Almost like they want it to happen."

Luc stared at her. "Well, *fuck them*," he said, filled with rage.

She tried a firm nod, mouthing *fuck them* silently.

His hand tightened on her belly. "*I want to talk about baby names*. This is *our* family, and we're going to be happy."

When her eyes held his, he knew that here was one of the things she needed from him, that he hadn't been giving her: solidarity, his strength, his ability to tell the world to go to hell. A real smile started to relax her mouth, and she wormed her hand around to find his and close firmly around it. "Lucie?" she suggested. "If it's a girl."

That made him so damn happy, just the thought of a little Lucie. Or Lucienne? "Summer doesn't work in French," he said, reaching up to play with her sunshine hair again. Plus, his babies were all bound to have dark hair and dark eyes. Yes, his genes would swamp those blue eyes and blondness she had, but maybe they would get her fine bones. "Maybe...Océane?"

Her face brightened. "I love that name."

"I guess we shouldn't rush quite so much into the next one, but you know I would really love to have both a Lucie and an Océane."

She pressed one hand to her stomach and held up the other in a warding gesture. "Let's get through this one first."

"Did you try the peanut butter?"

"Uh—"

"What about pretzels? Dom found pretzels suggested on a website."

"*Dom* did?"

"We were brainstorming." Luc shrugged.

She stared at him. "Is that what you guys were talking about the whole time? Food?"

"What else would we talk about?" he asked blankly.

So that's how she ended up laughing. And he ended up kissing her to get her to stop laughing at him. And then, and then...God, it felt so good to make love to her while she was laughing, to ease that silky top off, and that bra, and stroke her until the sparkle in her eyes got lost in hazy pleasure.

I can do this part, he thought, as he watched her, as he breathed in the scent of her arousal and his own surged through him. *I think I have this part down.*

It felt so damn good afterward to pull her in close to him, holding her as he fell asleep. As if he were a child pressing his face into a teddy-bear after a nightmare, breathing in a sweet, familiar scent and texture, all his worries just eased away. The last thing he remembered was her hand linking with his and the way all the tension seemed to leave her body in a soft sigh as she nestled between him and her pillow, falling asleep.

Chapter 22

" Patrice," a sandy voice said. Luc closed his hand around the little flower bracelet and looked around. "An excellent name for a baby. Or perhaps Patricia?"

It was five in the morning, but Luc had been fostered by a baker-pastry chef, and he had long since lost the ability to sleep in. Patrick pretended to be better at lazing around, but given that he was up at this hour of the morning even after a late night drinking, the façade was pretty see-through.

"Up early looking for waves?" Luc asked dryly.

Patrick peered at the flat pre-dawn sea below and gave a huge, aggravated sigh. "Damn Mediterranean. You couldn't have moved to Hawaii?"

"We talked about it."

"Yeah?" A quick glance. "Sarah and I, too."

Really. "But we thought the south of France was a good compromise." Sunshine, and enough of a clientele where he could still be one of the top chefs in the world.

"It's not too shabby," Patrick admitted. "Nice change from Paris."

Yeah, except he'd lost his *second* that way. "How's the engineering going?"

"Boring."

Luc blinked.

"There's no *speed* to it, the textures are all metal and computers and wire, there's no"—Patrick shoved his hands through his hair suddenly and flung them out—"*flavor.*"

Luc tightened his hand around the little bracelet and turned around.

"And *putain*, but it's slow. *Merde*, Luc. You have to sit still."

Luc took a careful moment before he spoke at all. It wasn't his place to hold Patrick back, clip his wings, discourage him from going for any dream he wanted to. He hadn't half-raised that kid to trap him in a cage. It wasn't in his nature to *ask for help* either, damn it. To expose the fact that he *needed* someone. But... "Well, if you get sick of it," he said very casually, "just let me know."

Another little silence. Luc carefully didn't look at Patrick at all, just gazed out at the dark Mediterranean. The stars were fading, a hint of color peeking over the horizon.

"Sarah doesn't want to work in a three-star kitchen," Patrick said.

"Really?" Luc said, utterly astonished. "But—she's *good*. She was born to work in a three-star kitchen."

Patrick smiled a little, in pleasure at the compliment to his fiancée. "You know, you could tell her that to her face once in a while, you bastard."

"I let her work in my kitchens!" Luc said incredulously. Hadn't they been through this once before? "How much clearer a compliment does she need?"

Patrick was starting to grin. "Women. Sometimes you just have to spell it out for them."

Oh, yes. Over and over and over.

But he kind of needed it spelled out for him, too.

"She could work for me here, while you do some of your engineering studies in the area, too," Luc said, very, very casually. "I mean—" He shrugged. "If you two want that option. She does need more training."

This smile was growing deeper and deeper on Patrick's face, all while Patrick wouldn't look at him, gazing downward. "Yeah? Is that an option for us?"

Luc shrugged. "Or...I don't know...I was thinking I might need to spend less time in the restaurant with fatherhood coming up. Might want to take on a partner." This weird thing was happening to Luc's cheeks. They felt...*hot*. Was he getting a fever? He touched them surreptitiously.

Patrick's eyebrows went up. "Not a *second*?"

"I've got another *second* these days." Luc sighed. "He needs a lot of work."

Patrick slipped his hands in his pockets and gazed at the Mediterranean oh-so-casually. "I like that chef de cuisine you found. Seems as if a man could have fun working with him."

Fun. Luc started to smile before he could stop it. See, that was what was missing from the kitchen now—Patrick's sense of fun.

Luc tightened his hand around the bracelet until its little jewels cut into his palm. Maybe he had learned the wrong lesson, a long time ago. Maybe everyone he loved *didn't* have to leave him. Maybe it didn't all have to melt, if someone didn't eat it fast enough.

"Be kind of fun to do a restaurant with two chefs. They could alternate menus and weeks, something like that. Two different takes around the season's fruits. And that way they could both have some kind of work-life balance. Or one of them could, you know, go to school part-time or something." Luc cleared his throat. "Personally I think I need to take a little bit more time off for the foreseeable future. Until my kids are all grown up, by which time I'll be..." His imagination failed him.

"Fifty," Patrick supplied. "At least."

Fifty.

Actually, good God, probably more like sixty, if he wanted several.

Basically, the second thirty years of his life.

"Wow," he said softly. "My life might be really, really different than what I thought it would be like, just last year."

"Congratulations," Patrick said, amused. And serious.

"Yeah," Luc said, more softly still. Wondering. As if he'd just blown gold powder over some dessert, making it all sparkly. He was afraid he would breathe too hard and screw it all up. So he held his breath and tried not to say anything at all, but then said, rough and tight: "It's just...she's going to need a godfather."

"Aww, hell." Patrick covered his heart with a fist, as if Luc had just hit him right there. "Really?"

Luc peeked again, just a subtle slanted glance, the way he would check people in his kitchens without them knowing it.

Patrick's eyes were shimmering. He lifted his other hand against Luc's glance, turning away a bit. "Give me a second." A flex and deliberate relaxation of Patrick's strong shoulders, hands dropping to hook thumbs in his jeans, and when he shifted back to face Luc, he could manage that lazy, easy shrug. "Good thing you asked me," he said offhandedly, as if this was all nothing to him. "Saves all that awkwardness when I had to nominate myself for the role. I mean, somebody has to make sure that kid is raised right."

"Yeah," Luc said. That was what he thought, too. "I...yeah."

One of those quick, blue looks of Patrick's that happened so fast and saw so deep, all while Patrick kept that lazy façade of his. "I was kidding about that."

But Luc just shook his head, his lungs so tight. "I don't know how," he said suddenly, low, to the terrace wall. "To raise a kid. To be a good dad. I've never even *seen* a good dad. And I don't have anything to *practice on.*"

Patrick's hands slid deep down into his jeans pockets. Out of the corner of his eye, Luc could see his throat flex as he swallowed. "Sarah thinks you did all right with me," he mentioned awkwardly, to the terrace wall, his lazy shrug completely failing to make him look indifferent or casual.

It shook the breath out of Luc. His throat tightened up, and...shit, his eyes were stinging. Patrick sometimes thought of him as his *father figure?* He was only four years older than Patrick. And he'd been such a desperately struggling teenager himself when he took Patrick on.

But...but Patrick had turned out all right, actually. More than all right. Patrick had turned into an exceptional man.

"I don't—I—" Luc rubbed the back of his neck. "I mean, I think you mostly raised yourself."

Patrick looked sideways at him. "Oh, you think that, do you?"

"Well..." Luc's shrug felt like some awkward imitation of one of Patrick's.

"All those apprentices you formed into top chefs who are now earning their own stars all over the world, they raised themselves, too, did they?"

"Well, I mean..."

"And those kids Jaime has you helping right now. The ones who are driving Sylvain crazy and you find easy to handle."

"That's all in the kitchens, Patrick. I don't even see kids until they're fifteen."

"Fine." Patrick shrugged, visibly pissed off. "All I'm saying is...you've had practice at parts of fatherhood, at least. And you seem to do pretty damn good at it. Now work with your wife, the one who loves to sit and teach little kids their letters all day as if that is something any person can do patiently, and I bet between you, the two of you can figure this out."

Really? Luc couldn't even start to encompass the softening of tension in him, that weird, shimmering thing that was happening to his heart, that the once screwed-up teenager he had tried so hard to raise right thought he would be a good father. "I think most of those apprentices that came through our kitchens owe a lot of their success to you, Patrick." This was no exaggeration. Patrick was fantastic at guiding new apprentices and even higher level chefs, at helping them survive and grow good at their impossible profession.

Patrick...was Patrick starting to flush, too? *Merde*, it was a good thing they were having this conversation at five in the morning where no one else could see them. "I'll tell you what," Patrick said. "I'll talk to Sarah. She's mentioned lately realizing she wants to spend more time working her way up in a good kitchen before she tries to do her own place. Maybe she and I could help out over the summer and see what she thinks of Provence. Help you and Summer get started."

"Yeah?" Luc couldn't help it. He beamed at that damn Mediterranean.

Patrick nodded slowly. "Luc. Just so you know. You were right to let yourself need people a little bit. You were right to call on friends."

Well, it had been for Summer, not for *him*, of course, but, but...he decided not to say that. Not to Patrick, who knew damn well that Luc had called on him.

And people had come, hadn't they? *Here we are. We're happy to help welcome your baby into the world.*

We know that sometimes being a good father, being a good husband, being a good person is tough to do entirely on your own.

He had a sudden, flashing vision of himself, Patrick, Sylvain, Dom, Gabriel, and Nico all gathered around a black-haired one-year-old with her face scrunched up at all their coaxing spoons. In the vision, Nico had pureed peaches spit back on his face. Luc grinned, and his hand opened slowly on the little flower bracelet, so that it lay, pretty and fragile in his callused palm but revealed to the world.

"What's that?" Patrick nodded at it but had far too great an instinct for what might be precious to reach for it.

"It's a present," Luc said. "It's for my daughter."

FIN

LAURA FLORAND

THANK YOU!

Thank you so much for reading! I hope you enjoyed Luc and Summer's story. And for December 2014 I'm working on a (free) short story about the birth of Luc and Summer's child as a little holiday present. Sign up for my newsletter to be emailed your own copy of the story when it's ready and to be kept abreast of other releases.

Speaking of new releases, the first half of 2015 will see the launch of my new Vie en Roses series with Once Upon a Rose as well as another book in the Amour et Chocolat series, which takes you back to a well-loved place in Paris with a hero and heroine I am very attached to! Keep reading for glimpses.

Meanwhile, make sure to catch the other books in the Amour et Chocolat series. You can find the story of Luc and Summer's tempestuous courtship in *The Chocolate Heart* and Patrick and Sarah's story in *The Chocolate Temptation*. Dom and Jaime's story is in *The Chocolate Touch*, Sylvain and Cade's in *The Chocolate Thief*, and Gabriel and Jolie's in *The Chocolate Rose*. Keep reading for a glimpse of *The Chocolate Temptation* as well as a complete book list.

Thank you so much for sharing this world with me! For some behind-the-scenes glimpses of the research with top chefs and chocolatiers, check out my website and Facebook page. I hope to meet up with you there!

Thank you and all the best,

Laura Florand
Website: www.lauraflorand.com
Twitter: @LauraFlorand
Facebook: www.facebook.com/LauraFlorandAuthor
Newsletter: www.lauraflorand.com/newsletter/

LAURA FLORAND

ONCE UPON A ROSE, EXCERPT

It's the start of a new series! Set in Provence, in the south of France, La Vie en Roses series takes us into the heart of a powerful family in the perfume industry and into the hearts of the five male cousins who are its heirs. Here's a glimpse of Matthieu Rosier, the rising family patriarch, in his valley full of roses...and the American upstart who just stole a chunk of his land.

"You still have the key," Layla said.

Matt braced his hands on the doorjamb, on either side of her above her head. *That* moved him into her space—caging her in the size of him, and all his body wide open to her. But of course, she could always take one step back and just shut the door. "It's in my back pocket," he said. That little smile as he held her eyes, and that deep, deep voice. God, a smile was a gorgeous look on him. She wanted to play with it, run her fingers over it, nurture it. "And I think my hands are dirty."

His jeans looked as if they'd been through a lot more than dirty hands. And, anyway, he'd just wiped his hands off so carefully she'd been *sure* he was about to touch her with them. But now they gripped the doorjamb above her, not touching her at all.

Meaning she would have to touch him, if she wanted any touching to occur.

His *back* pocket. Her palm itched to slide over the curve of that taut butt. "If I—if I got it out, what would you do?"

The biceps to either side of her face grew more pronounced. He gazed down at her, eyes not grumpy at all, oddly quiet. Intent. "What would you want me to do?" His voice didn't boom. It slid over her, textured, strong and rich, entirely reassuring.

"N—nothing," she admitted. Well, kind of that was what she wanted. With, like, the only two neurons that seemed to be functioning in her brain right now that was what she wanted. The other two hundred billion seemed to want something entirely different.

Evidently a big, hot body that smelled of roses short-circuited all synapses.

His low, deep voice rubbed over her. "Well, I guess I'm going to do nothing, then."

Oh, really? Would you really do that for me? Hold all that big, aggressive need to do still for me?

He tightened his hands on the doorjamb. "I told you, it's not that easy to do."

But he waited, quite still except for the flexing of his arm muscles.

She slid her hand into his back pocket slow, slow, slow, afraid of what she was doing but tantalized by it, too, by that firm curve, by the warmth and snugness of the pocket, by the arms framing her that hardened and didn't move. By his eyes watching her. Intent and pushing his will on her, as if he knew exactly what he wanted to do to her, but maybe this hint of caution, too, as if he wasn't quite sure what she might do to him.

She came out with the key, iron and warm, but she didn't step back into the house with it and shut the door. She stared up at him, liking her little space inside the cage of his body so much she could have stayed there for an hour, just with that warmth so carefully not touching her.

He took a deep breath and sighed it out. "I promised to do nothing, didn't I?"

She nodded mutely.

Another huff of a breath, and he shoved himself away from the doorjamb and her. "Well, that was even harder than I expected."

He picked up his toolkit and studied her another long moment, as if she was really hard to figure out. "I don't believe we've been properly introduced yet," he said slowly and held out his hand. "I'm Matthieu Rosier."

Her hand disappeared into his, slim and strong but engulfed by his strength and size. "Layla Dubois."

He didn't release her hand. "You stole my land," he said, still studying her as if something here was a complete mystery to him.

"It was a gift."

"I want it back."

Yeah, but now that she knew what it was like to be here, sheltered and private and far away from any thought of media or performance, she didn't want to get kicked back out into the world. The same way her hand, warm and snug inside his, didn't want to be released. "The thing is...I like it here."

She expected that flare of grouchiness on his part at her refusal, but instead a little light came into in his eyes, as if she had paid him a compliment. "Do you?"

She gestured out over the roses with her free hand. "It's beautiful."

The light in his eyes grew brighter. "You really think so?"

She nodded.

His hand didn't seem to know how to let go of hers. But then, she didn't try to wiggle free either. It was such a nice, strong, warm hold.

"I'll try to take good care of it," she offered. "I won't sell it to the highest bidder or anything."

A hint of brooding snuck back into his expression. "The highest bidder is likely to be one of my cousins. They have more liquid assets."

Not having ever had an extended family, she had no idea how to address that. "And you can keep picking my roses."

That made his head rear back. "Of course I can keep picking those roses!" he growled. "We just planted those bushes three years ago, they—" He broke off as she shook her head, laughing silently at him.

"Or you *could* say, 'Thank you very much for being so cooperative,'" she suggested sternly.

He studied her, one eyebrow going up. Then he leaned a tad into her, pressing his will onto her and seeing how she held up to it. "I could say that. But they are *my* roses."

Ha, as if he was the first man who'd ever tried to get her to bend to his sheer force of male will. Busking around Europe and then dealing with the music industry had brought her into contact with plenty of men who wanted the little female to cooperate. Little females who couldn't afford a personal bodyguard had to learn how to look out for themselves in the world. So she just raised her eyebrows, amused. "Every single last petal?"

"Every single one."

"You're very possessive, aren't you?"

He nodded unhesitatingly, as if she had just affirmed one of his more admirable qualities.

"I'm pretty hard to hold." Maybe she was changing the subject from roses to herself, but that was fair, wasn't it? To make sure he knew that she was just fooling around, to make sure that they were on the same page about that?

He looked down at his hand, currently holding hers so easily and surely, and made the slightest moue of disagreement.

For some reason, that made a tingle run through her. "I'm tired of other people trying to own me," she tried to explain.

His hand squeezed once, strong and gentle both, around hers. "'Holding' and 'owning' aren't the same thing." He released her hand. "*Bonne nuit,* Layla."

"*Bonne nuit.*"

He got maybe ten paces before he glanced back over his shoulder and sent her a wicked little smile. "I meant it, by the way. My door's unlocked."

***

Once Upon a Rose, coming early 2015! Sign up for my newsletter (http://lauraflorand.com/newsletter/) to be notified when it's released.

ONCE A HERO, EXCERPT

An Amour et Chocolat novel

Célie worked in heaven. Every day she ran up the stairs to it, into the light that reached down to her, shining through the great casement windows as she came into the *laboratoire*, gleaming in soft dark tones off the marble counters. She hung up her helmet and her black leather jacket, and she pulled on her black chef's jacket instead, and she ran her fingers through her hair to spike it back up, and washed her hands, and stroked one palm all down the length of one long marble counter as she headed to check on her chocolates from the day before. Oh, the beauties. There they were, the flat, perfect squares with their little prints, all subtle and adamant, the way Dominique Richard liked them. Perfect. There was the ganache and the praliné setting up in its metal frames. That was the third day on the mint ganache. Time to pull the *guitare* down off the wall and slice that mint ganache into those little perfect squares and send those to the enrober.

She called teasing hellos to everyone as she crossed them or they arrived: "What, you here already, Amand? I didn't expect you until noon." Totally unfair to the hardworking caramellier, but he had slept in once, after a birthday bash, arriving to work so late and so horrified at himself that no one had ever let him forget it.

"Dom, when's the wedding again?" Dom Richard, their boss, was diligently trying to resist marrying his girlfriend until he had given her enough time to figure out what a bad bet he was, and the only way to handle that was tease him. Otherwise Célie's heart might squeeze too much in this warm, fuzzy, mushy urge to give the man a big hug—and then a very hard shove into the arms of his happiness.

Guys who screwed a woman's chance at happiness over because they were so convinced they weren't good enough did *not* earn any points in her book.

Like, *fuck them. Maybe I wasn't good enough either and could have used you around.*

"Can somebody work around here besides me?" Dom asked in complete exasperation, totally unmerited, just because the guy had no idea how to deal with all the teasing that came his way. It was why they couldn't resist. He was so big, and he got all ruffled and grouchy and adorable.

"I want to have time to pick out my dress!" Célie protested, hauling down the *guitare.* "I know exactly what you two are going to do. You'll put it off until all the sudden you wander in some Monday with a stunned, scared look on your face, and we'll find out you eloped over the weekend to some village in Côte d'Ivoire. And we'll have missed the whole thing!"

Dom growled desperately, like a persecuted bear, and bent his head over his éclairs.

Célie grinned and started slicing her mint ganache into squares, the guitar wires cutting through it effortlessly. *There you go.* She tasted one. Soft, dissolving in her mouth, delicately infused with fresh mint. *Mmm. Perfect. Time to get it all dressed up.* Enrobing time.

She got to spend her days like that. In one of the top chocolate *laboratoires* in Paris. Okay, the top, but some people over in the Sixth like a certain Sylvain Marquis persisted in disputing that point. What*ever.* He was such a classicist. *Bor*ing. And *everyone* knew that cinnamon did not marry well with dark chocolate, so that latest Cade Marquis bar of his was just ridiculous.

And she didn't even want to think about Simon Casset with his stupid sculptures. So he could do fancy sculptures. Was that real chocolate? Did people eat that stuff? No. So. *She* did important chocolate. Chocolate that adventured. Chocolate people wanted to sink their teeth into. Chocolate that opened a whole world out in front of a person, right there in her mouth.

Chocolate that was so much beyond anything she had ever dreamed her life would be as a teenager that...*God*, she loved her day. She stretched out her arms, nearly bopped their apprentice Véro who was carrying a bowl of chocolate to the scale, grinned at her in apology, and carried her mint ganaches over to the enrober.

She'd been loving her day for a little over three hours and was getting kind of ready to take a little break from doing so and let her back muscles relax for fifteen minutes when Guillemette showed up at the top of the stairs. Célie cocked her eyebrows at the other woman hopefully. Time for a little not-smoke break, perhaps? Were things quiet enough downstairs? Célie didn't smoke anymore, since some stupid guy she once knew made her quit and she found out how many *flavors* there were out there when they weren't being hidden by tobacco. But sometimes she'd give about anything to be able to hold a cigarette between her fingers and blow smoke out with a sexy purse of her lips and truly believe that was all it took to make her cool.

Because the double ear piercings and the spiky hair were a lot less expensive over the long-term, but they could be misinterpreted as bravado, whereas—

A teenager slouching against a wall and blowing smoke from her mouth was *always* clearly genuine coolness, no bravado about it, of course. Célie rolled her eyes at herself, and Guillemette, instead of gesturing for her to come join her for the not-smoke break, instead came up to her counter where she was working and stole a little chocolate. "There's a guy here to see you," Guillemette said a little doubtfully. "And we're getting low on the Arabica."

Célie glanced at the trolley full of trays where the Arabica chocolates had finished and were ready to be transferred to metal flats. "I'll bring some down with me. Who's the guy?" Maybe that guy she had met Saturday, Danny and Tiare's friend? She tried to figure out if she felt any excitement about that, but adrenaline ran pretty high in her on a normal day in the *laboratoire,* so it was hard to tell.

"He didn't say."

And Guillemette hadn't asked? Maybe there had been several customers at once or something.

"I'll be down in a second," Célie said, and Guillemette headed back while Célie loaded up a couple of the metal flats they used in the display cases with the Arabica, with its subtle texture, no prints on this one. Dark and exotic and touched with coffee.

She ran down the spiral metal stairs with her usual happy energy, and halfway down, the face of the big man waiting with his hands in his pockets by the pastry display counter came into view, and she—

Tripped.

The two trays flew out of her hands as her foot caught on one of the metal steps, and she grabbed after them even as they sailed away. One tray knocked against her hand as she tried to grab it, and chocolates shot out of it, raining down everywhere just as she started to realize she was falling, too.

Oh, *fuck,* that instant flashing realization of how much this was going to hurt and how much too late it was to save herself, even as she tried to grab the banister, and—

Hard hands caught her, and she *oofed* into them and right up against a big body, like she was a rugby ball, except it was raining chocolates during this game, and she used to know someone who was really good at rugby, and—

She gasped for breath, post-impact, and pulled herself upright, staring up at the person who still held her in steadying hands. A man who had once been really good at rugby.

Wary, hard, intense hazel green eyes stared back down at her. He looked caught, instead of her, his lips parted, as if maybe he had meant to say something. But, looking down at her, he didn't say anything at all.

Strong eyebrows, strong stubborn forehead and cheekbones and chin—every single damn bone in his body stubborn—and skin so much more tanned and weathered than when she had last seen it. Dark brown hair cropped military-close to his head and sanded by sun.

Célie wrenched back out of his hands, her own flying to her face as she burst into tears.

Just—burst. Right there in public, with all her colleagues and their customers around her. She backed up a step and then another, tears flooding down her cheeks, chocolate crushing under her feet.

"Célie," he said, and even his voice sounded rougher and tougher. And wary.

She turned and ran back up the stairs, dashing at her eyes to try to see the steps through the tears, and burst back up through the glass doors into the *laboratoire*. Dom looked up immediately, and then straightened. "Célie? *What's wrong?*" Big, bad Dom, yeah, right, with the heart of gold. He came forward while she shook her head, having nothing she could tell him, scrubbing at her eyes in vain.

The glass door behind her opened. "Célie," that rough, half-familiar voice said. "I—"

She darted toward the other end of the *laboratoire* and her ganache cooling room.

"Get the fuck out of my kitchen," Dom said behind her, flat, and she paused, half-turning.

Dom Richard, big and dark, stood blocking the other man in the glass doorway. Joss locked eyes with him, these two big dangerous men, one who wanted in and one who wasn't about to let him. Célie bit a finger, on sudden fear, and started back toward them.

Joss Castel looked past Dom to her. Their eyes held.

"Célie, go in the other room," Dom said without turning around. And to Joss: "You. *Get out.*"

Joss thrust his hands in his pockets. Out of combat. Sheathing his weapons. He nodded once, a jerk of his head, at Célie, and turned and made his way down the stairs.

Dom followed. Célie went to the casement window above the store's entrance, and watched as Joss left the store, crossed the street, and turned to look up at the window. She started crying again, just at that look, and when she lifted her hand to dash it across her eyes, he must have caught the movement through the reflection off the glass, because his gaze focused on her.

"What was that all about?" Dom asked behind her. She turned, but she couldn't quite get herself to leave the window. She couldn't quite get herself to walk out of sight. "Célie, who is that guy and what did he do?"

She shook her head.

"Célie."

She slashed a hand through the air, wishing she could shut things down like a *man* could, make her hand say, *This subject is closed.* When *Dom* slashed a subject closed with one move of his hand like that, no one messed with *him*. Well, except for her, of course. "Just someone I knew before. Years ago. Before I worked here."

"When you lived in Créteil?" Their old, bad *banlieue.* "And he was bad? Did he hit you? Was he dealing? What was it?"

She gazed at Dom uneasily. For all he was so big and bad and dark, always seeming to have that threat of violence in him, it was the first time she had ever seen him about to commit violence.

"No," she said quickly. "No. He didn't."

"Célie."

"No, he really didn't, damn it, Dom! *Merde.* Do you think I would *let* him?"

"You couldn't have been over eighteen."

"Yeah, well—he didn't."

Dom's teeth showed, like a man who didn't believe her and was about to reach out and rip the truth out of her. "Then *what—*"

"He left me! That's all. He fucking left me there, so that he could go make himself into a better person. Yeah. So *fuck you*, Dom. Go marry your girlfriend instead of playing around with this *I-need-to-be-good-enough* shit and leave me alone!"

And she sank down on her butt, right there in the cooling room, between the trolleys full of trayed chocolate and the marble island, in the slanting light from the casement window, and cried.

Just cried and cried and cried.

It sure as hell put a damper on chocolate production for a while, but for as long as she needed it, people did leave her alone.

***

Once a Hero, coming 2015! Sign up for my newsletter (http://lauraflorand.com/newsletter/) to be notified of its release.

LAURA FLORAND

OTHER BOOKS BY LAURA FLORAND

Snow Queen Duology

Snow-Kissed (a novella)

Sun-Kissed (also part of the Amour et Chocolat series)

Amour et Chocolat Series

All's Fair in Love and Chocolate, a novella in *Kiss the Bride*

The Chocolate Thief

The Chocolate Kiss

The Chocolate Rose (also part of La Vie en Roses series)

The Chocolate Touch

The Chocolate Heart

The Chocolate Temptation

Sun-Kissed (also a sequel to *Snow-Kissed*)

Shadowed Heart (a sequel to *The Chocolate Heart*)

La Vie en Roses Series

Turning Up the Heat (a novella)

The Chocolate Rose (also part of the Amour et Chocolat series)

SHADOWED HEART

A Rose in Winter, a novella in *No Place Like Home*

Once Upon a Rose (upcoming)

Memoir

Blame It on Paris

ACKNOWLEDGEMENTS

I am deeply grateful, as always, to Laurent Jeannin, executive pastry chef of Michelin three-star L'Épicure, at Le Bristol, Paris, and to Éric Frechon, executive head chef, for allowing me to research in their kitchens.

While deciding what to do with this unusual story— a sequel to a happily ever after story—many, many writers and readers came forward to offer to beta read for me and encouraged me to publish it. I want to thank from the bottom of my heart all of those who offered, and particularly Stephanie Burgis, Barbara Morgenroth, April White, Lynn Latimer, Mercy and Dale Anderson, Sydney Nolan, and Shannon O'Shea Schmeig. Their feedback was invaluable.

And a huge thank you, of course, goes to all my readers for your investment in these books and these characters. I'm so glad that they speak to you.

ABOUT LAURA FLORAND

Laura Florand burst on the contemporary romance scene in 2012 with her award-winning Amour et Chocolat series. Her international bestselling books have been translated into seven languages, been named among the Best Books of the Year by *Romantic Times* and Barnes & Noble, received the RT Seal of Excellence and starred reviews from *Publishers Weekly, Library Journal,* and *Booklist,* and been recommended by NPR, *USA Today,* and *The Wall Street Journal,* among others.

After a Fulbright year in Tahiti and backpacking everywhere from New Zealand to Greece, and several years living in Madrid and Paris, Laura now teaches Romance Studies at Duke University. Contrary to what the "Romance Studies" may imply, this means she primarily teaches French language and culture and does a great deal of research on French gastronomy, particularly chocolate.

LAURA FLORAND

COPYRIGHT

Copyright 2014, Laura Florand

Cover by Sebastien Florand

ISBN-13: 978-0-9885065-8-9

CPSIA information can be obtained at www.ICGtesting.com
Printed in the USA
LVOW07s1704260215

428501LV00004B/304/P

9 780988 506589